Love Under the Stars

J.M. Guilfoyle

ADDITIONAL WORKS BY J.M. GUILFOYLE

Contemporary Fantasy

Darkspell: Justice

Romance

Christmas Confessions

Writing Journey Anthologies

Denizens of the Deep
Triple Vision
Masks, Facades, and Reveals

DEDICATION

For my son. Autism isn't something to be ashamed of.

CONTENTS

LOVE UNDER THE STARS

CHAPTER ONE

WHO DOESN'T LOVE SPACE ZOMBIES?

Ellie

Cosmic Contagion!

Signs had been plastered in the front window of The Inkwell for weeks. It was the biggest event at their small bookstore all year. And every time she passed the store, Ellie never *once* noticed that it was a ticketed event until someone mentioned it to a friend heading into the Inkwell. Literally a few moments ago! She was *sure* no sign on the front of the store said anything about tickets!

Meet Jackson Wolfe!

She'd been moving around plans for weeks. Ellie found a replacement teacher for the art class at Making Spirits Bright, the small shop where she worked at night. As if she hadn't spent all day teaching some elementary children of their town in art class (and tonight was an event at the school, which getting that covered was even more challenging), Ellie spent her nights teaching their adults how to paint a whole painting in 2 hours.

As she stood staring at the sign in the front window again, she scanned the whole thing from top to bottom, bottom to top, left to right, and so on. No mention of tickets!

Ellie ripped open the front door and made a beeline for the reading area in the back. The Inkwell was cramped, but it had a small cafe that turned into whatever they needed — Ellie had learned over the years to avoid slam poetry night at all costs. During slam poetry nights, desperation from The Inkwell's owner led him to occasionally pluck unsuspecting shoppers to make up poetry on the spot.

Inside, at the makeshift barricade created by newly moved bookshelves and tables, the *Cosmic Contagion* signing event sign included a 'tickets sold out' banner across the poster.

"Sold out?" Ellie roared, calling all the attention to her as people started filing in for the signing.

A few snickers made Ellie's cheeks bright red.

Jessie, a guy in his late 20s like Ellie, hair so dark it was impossible to tell if it was black or brown in the bookstore's low light, popped his lips behind her. "Didn't you... get a ticket?"

"Would I be pissed if I got a ticket?" Ellie growled.

"You're always here preordering and getting special editions of..."

Of every single one of Jackson Wolfe's books? Yes! She knew that! When she had money, of course.

Ellie ran her fingers through her delicate waves. Her plain brown hair spilled over her hands and face. "Tell me you reserved one... or someone called in and said they couldn't come and give their ticket to..."

"El?" Jesse said and patted her shoulder. "I'm sorry. It's been sold out for..."

"No!" Ellie whined, now pushing her hair back so she could see again. Each book she'd brought weighed down the canvas bag on her shoulder like dead weight.

"Sorry, El. Maybe you can ask one of the guys coming in? Someone might have an extra ticket, or if you sweet talk enough..."

But there were already enough men smirking at her. With this crowd, there would be no way she wasn't recognizable. Her once-a-year third job made sure of that. "That seems like a bad idea."

Their town wasn't huge, but it wasn't too small either. The population that attended places like Mighty Con, though? That was pretty darn consistent. Ellie had seen all these guys at the convention for years. The first year was fun... but these guys were becoming less congenial as the years continued on. And the rumors spread.

"*Poser,*" one of their jibes made it through the growing crowd's noise. Sam, The Inkwell's owner, gathered tickets for the event at the cobbled-together entrance.

Ellie pulled out a copy of Wolfe's last book before *Cosmic Contagion*, which sat atop her pile in her bag. *Epidemic of the Damned*. Only out for a year, and Ellie had broken the spine in multiple places; the front and back covers were bent and folded, dog-eared. It was one of many well-loved books in her collection. She *should* purchase a new copy for Jackson Wolfe to sign, but... well, there was only so much money in her account, and Mighty Con was just around the corner with a new cosplay she needed to finish...

Turning, Ellie knew she'd already overstayed her welcome. More words were about to be hurled her way based on the deep, menacing glares she garnered. But when she turned, a person stood there, silent, stoic, and staring. She'd have run into him if she weren't paying attention. The guy blended in with the rest of the crowd, but stood slightly apart from everyone else. Floppy dark blond hair with erratic curls at the end, which flipped up in various directions. Slight build. A dark red polo shirt over a long-sleeved shirt and jeans, paired with dirty Chucks. He also had a cross-body bag — though his bag wasn't covered in paint and other art mediums and not weighed down by nearly as many books.

"I have a ticket," the guy said quietly.

"Great. Way to rub it in," Ellie muttered.

"See, there you go!" Jesse tried being helpful, but it took all of Ellie's willpower not to smack him on the head. "Problem solved."

"I can't take that from you. You go," Ellie said, then pushed past the guy who looked much younger than her, except for the Ashworth Laboratory ID clipped to his belt loop.

"It's an extra ticket. I was supposed to have a date."

The tone of his voice caught her before the words themselves. He was relatively monotone, and when Ellie made eye contact, he held it but fidgeted uncomfortably.

"Really. It's fine," Ellie sighed.

So far tonight, she'd been called worse things than 'poser', and people already thought she took advantage of them when she never did such a thing in her life... If she accepted the ticket in front of all these guys, everything everyone said about her in the Mighty Con group would explode as if it were confirmation of all the things they had said about her.

The guy continued staring; hand held out with the slightly crumpled ticket. "You're a fan of Jackson Wolfe's books, yes?"

"Yes," Ellie sighed and folded the book in her hands dangerously. New creases were surely forming on the front cover.

"Reach out your hand, take the ticket, El," Jesse prodded her.

"OOOH! The Mighty Con's mighty whore is at it again!"

Ah, there it was. Ellie sighed.

In the past, this treatment used to not start until men approached her. They'd assume she would say yes to anything, and when she rejected them, the names began within seconds. Now, these guys wouldn't wait for her to reject them... the name-calling started on sight tonight. But Ellie also couldn't stomach walking all the way through the line of people, the friends of friends of friends, and their angry gawking with name calling.

"Thank you," Ellie answered softly, turned on her heels, shuffled straight for Sam, the crowd parting to let her by. God, she was practically plague ridden. Ellie jammed the ticket at Sam.

There were four rows of seats, each with five seats. Again, not huge, except for The Inkwell, where a crowd of over twenty could be considered a fire hazard.

Ellie took an end seat in the second row, hoping it would make for an easy escape if need be. Her leg bounced nervously, and she unfolded the book again, staring at the beat-up cover in her lap.

"Look what the pathetic zombie dragged in." Anthony turned in the chair in front of hers.

Damn it!

Her ex — or whatever a guy was considered if they only went on a single date. Anthony had always been the cute guy at the con. The kind she'd never thought went to conventions because they were for 'geeks' and all the stupid excuses people made.

"Maybe she's here to eat our brains..." Another familiar voice, Carlos's deep timbre, chimed in. Carlos and his smooth, thick black hair and rich, dark eyes were the kind women fell over at the con table. But he had that geeky air, so Carlos never felt out of place at Mighty Con. None of the other women she'd worked with at the cons cared about actually attending the con, but they cared about seeing Carlos daily.

Carlos tilted his head at her paint-stained clothes. "Maybe not dressed like *that*."

"Ay, man! Get it right!" The third haunted Ellie. High school rival and all-around asshole, Derek. "She's here to get enough to hawk. Clearly, Ellie needs the money to get into Mighty Con so she can *con* another guy into bed..."

Floppy hair broke through the conversation, literally passing between Ellie and the chair in front of her and he took the seat next to her when he could have still had almost any other seat. Although the seats were filling up fast. "She's a fan of Jackson Wolfe," floppy hair said, his nose plastered in a pristine copy of *Cosmic Contagion*.

Chapter Two

MAYBE NO TICKET IS BETTER THAN HAVING A TICKET

Ellie

"Dude," Carlos smirked and pointed at the guy next to Ellie. "I've seen you before."

"Yeah..." Anthony's long, drawn-out agreement at least took the spotlight off Ellie for the time being. "You ask all those super in-depth questions at Mighty Con."

Floppy hair treated Carlos and Anthony like the insignificant specks they should be, and kept his nose to the book when he answered, "Disappointingly, most creators don't remember what their consultants correct on the page. There is a disturbing lack of basic scientific knowledge as well."

Ellie kept her head down, trying not to smile at each guy's slack-jawed face.

It didn't last long.

"Oh! So, you found someone new to cheat out of an upgrade, Mighty..."

Ellie slammed her foot into Carlos' chair hard enough to shut him up.

The guy next to her simply turned the page of his book and answered in the same flat, monotone-ish manner, "I gave Eleanor the ticket because she's a fan of Jackson Wolfe."

And then it hit her. Ellie's entire body went ice cold. "How do you know my name?" Because she certainly hadn't said it. Had he been listening to her and Jesse talk for that long? Did Jessie say her name? No, Jessie called her El, not Eleanor. El could be short for plenty of other names. Ellen, Elizabeth...

"Eleanor Chapman. Cosplay artist and model for VFX make-up artist..."

"How do you know that?" Her breath hitched. Had she just accepted a ticket from someone who'd stalked her at conventions? She'd heard stories that were usually a 'friend of a friend of a friend' and so on about this happening.

"Your name is listed in the convention program. Has been for the last four years. Along with Bethany Roberts and Michaela Harmon."

That was true. Michaela and Bethany had worked the VFX booth for several years now.

Either way, this new information sent Carlos into a tizzy. "Oh! The Mighty Whore has a fanboy!"

Setting his book down, floppy hair scrunched up his face at Carlos and Anthony's eternally annoying laughter. "I have..."

"Oh, what? You one of those 'I have an eidetic memory' bullshit..."

"I had an eidetic memory as a child," floppy hair answered. "But eidetic memory is not what most people think. It's not recalling information but an actual photographic image and only lasts for several seconds and..."

Ellie thought to keep herself, like floppy hair had been previously, in the folds of her crumpled book because maybe if Carlos' attention were diverted, she could sit in blissful quiet until the reading and signing started.

Floppy hair continued, "I was about to say that I read every Mighty Con program book. It's hard to miss the same name several years in a row."

Another chair dropped into the aisle next to Ellie, and a man sat beside her with brown curls — purposely messy but in a charming way — falling into his eyes. "This the girlfriend?"

Eyes back to being firmly planted in his copy of *Cosmic Contagion,* floppy hair responded, "I don't have a girlfriend. But my date decided we were not optimal for each other at the last minute."

"Oh," the new guy whined.

Then Ellie dared to take a good look at the guy and immediately regretted it because she chirped.

"So, who's this?"

"Eleanor..."

"Ellie," she stupidly corrected, now wringing her book more than she had been before. Even stupider because she couldn't hide behind a rolled book as easily as one splayed open while pretending to read. But then she saw him, and there was no way to *unsee* him! Jackson Wolfe sat next to her. Messy, curls and all. Holy crap.

"I think the *lovely* woman prefers to be called Ellie, Zack. You should take note," Jackson smirked.

"Noted," Floppy Hair — Zack, apparently — shoved the book he'd been reading across Ellie and into Jackson's face. "You didn't take all my notes into account. Explain."

"He always forgets the 'please,'" Jackson then attempted to cause a heart attack by nudging Ellie. "Not every note *you* give me helps tell the story. Sometimes, I need to take a little creative license."

"This is absolutely inaccurate," Zack muttered, flipping to the next page. But just as suddenly, he shoved the book across again, and — again — Jackson pushed Zack's hand and the book back.

"So, back to the female matter at hand." A little wave sent concerning flutters through Ellie's chest, but Jackson continued, "What happened to your date *exactly*?"

"I'd rather not discuss it."

"Then where did your other ticket go?"

"Eleanor," Zack paused to correct himself. "Ellie needed a ticket."

"She did?"

Oh sure, intense scrutiny from Ellie's *favorite* author was just what she needed.

"She's a fan of yours. Explain how you got to this because scientifically..."

"No. And I can see she's a fan. I think we need to find you another copy of *Epidemic of the Damned*. That one's seen better days."

"Um," Ellie's dumb brain couldn't form a sentence, but somehow Jackson Wolfe caught on.

"*Zachary*," Jackson pulled out a boyishly charming smile, then continued, "is my scientific consultant."

"I question why you pay me when you don't take my notes seriously."

"*I told you*, I take them seriously until they don't help tell the story." Someone at the front of the crowd started waving Jackson to them, angrily jabbing the watch on his wrist. "I'm sorry to keep talking over you. It's absolutely astounding to meet you. If I don't start this shindig, my manager might turn me into a zombie." Before he left, Jackson added in the most unsubtle way, "She's cute. Ask her out."

Without taking his eyes off the novel, Zack said, "And he questions my clarity in statements. Where would I ask you out to? We don't even know each other."

"Dude, Mighty Whore might've just caught a break," Carlos chimed in quietly.

In probably the most un-Eleanor Chapman move ever, Ellie kicked Carlos' seat with all her might and hissed, "Stop being an asshole, Carlos! Just because I always reject you doesn't mean you can be a dick to other guys."

"Really?" Carlos laughed. "Him? You're attracted to a guy like *him*?"

She gave Zack one more look and smiled. Unlike Carlos and Anthony, Zack wasn't a gym bro. He was fit enough under layers of baggy shirts and his jeans. But there was still the awkward lank and weight. If Zack was strong, he wasn't built. And Ellie realized he was probably older than he looked and had a 'baby face.'

Keeping her head, Ellie didn't throw her crumpled book at Carlos' head like she daydreamed about. Instead, her mind came up with a different, appropriate reaction. "Yes. Him."

Zack

Weird. Creepy. Geek.

Oh, great. Those words were swirling around Zack's head again. The guys sitting in front of him and Ellie kept giggling and glancing back. Even with reading, he heard everything. Felt their prying eyes.

The judging.

It was pain, like the attention stabbed into Zack's eyes with each darting glance.

Also, each page of *Cosmic Contagion* stabbed Zack in the brain with its scientific inaccuracy.

But when one guy laughed, Zack squirmed. Next to him, Ellie grinned at Jackson in the same lovesick manner most women did. Once, though, she glanced at Zack; her smile for him looked reserved, and she whispered, "Thank you."

And that's when Zack noticed Jackson. Adding to the unnerving amount of attention, making Zack's insides twist. Because Jackson was right. If cute was easily defined (which Zack never thought it was), he might consider Ellie cute. And cute girls never said anything other than Zack was 'cute.' Then those girls typically proceeded to pursue Jackson.

Ellie

Ellie felt her... everything get hot and sweaty. Jackson Wolfe's reading included approximately 1000% more glancing in her direction than she'd ever thought possible. Not that she felt like Jackson was flirting with her. But that didn't stop his attention from making Ellie more flustered than ever.

And Jackson's curious glances didn't do anything to *his* reading, which was as flawless as its author.

Next to Ellie, Zack's eyes flew over the pages, reading silently while his apparent friend finished his own passage. Zack's minute expressions were funnier to watch than Jackson's reading. Mostly, they were annoyed at something Jackson had written; occasionally, his mouth would silently form words, and then he'd purse his lips and scowl.

"I'd love to take a few questions," Jackson's smooth voice carried over the crowd, and immediately, hands were in the air.

Including Zack's.

"Not you," Jackson waved off his friend.

"But you seem..."

"Ask *Ellie*." Jackson's grin and nod turned more than half the audience towards them. Ellie sunk into her chair. "Not me."

With all his seriousness, Zack responded, "She will not understand your motivation. And, frankly, neither do I."

This garnered a few laughs from the crowd that quickly died away when Jackson called on another fan.

Not that that stopped Zack from complaining. "It doesn't make sense. I told him how viruses operate."

"Art isn't always logical," Ellie whispered.

"Yes, it is. Art is very logical. It follows the shapes of the world. Recreated curves and shadows. It's more logical than most believe. You understand; you make art."

She would have asked how he knew, but considering how covered in paint most of her belongings were, it wouldn't take a grade A detective to figure out she was an artist. Digging in her bag, Ellie found her most tattered Jackson Wolfe book. She had several copies of *Zombie Wasteland* and found the book inspired some of her personal art. Ellie had started the sacrilegious sketching inside the book last year. She found herself covering pages in art, depicting the scenes in the book, which did nothing but distort the book further.

Page 114 contained the picture she searched for. A zombie bathed in neon pink light and purple shadows.

"Colors don't appear like this in the real world. Usually, photos you see with this lighting are all staged or enhanced. Painting this isn't logical."

"It is re-creatable..."

"Re-creatable, yes, but like I said... artificial."

"Lovebirds?" Jackson cooed. "Shhh. Or take it outside."

After a sharp inhale, Zack stated very matter-of-factly, "You told me to ask her. And I did."

It took everything in Ellie not to laugh at Jackson *freaking* Wolfe's stunned face.

CHAPTER THREE

SAY NO TO CONFRONTATION

Ellie

When Jackson Wolfe's manager stopped him from taking more fan questions, the author called Zack to talk with him as he signed books rather than continue their conversation — or spirited debate, as Jackson called it — in a more civilized manner. The queue formed faster than Ellie could think, and she ended up at the very end.

The end of the line suited her just fine. Ellie dug through her bag, frowning at each Wolfe book she removed. None were in good — or even fair — condition. Certainly not worthy of being signed or even seen by the author. Unfortunately, her bank account wouldn't allow for more book purchases right now. Not if she wanted a half-decent cosplay for Mighty Con.

It was down to two battered book candidates when she recognized Zack's voice again.

"Your rewrite of the dispersal mechanism is nothing like the draft you sent me."

Jackson sighed. "My editor said it needed to be more dramatic. It's exciting."

"It's filled with more inaccuracies per page than anywhere else in the book. A dispersal in the ventilation shafts wouldn't work like this. Airflow patterns would…"

"Whoa," Jackson breathed and stared at Ellie's hands. Or rather, the two books in her hand. "That's some heavy-duty love going on with those books. So much it might be a crime." He flashed her another witty smile, and there went Ellie's brain again. She dumped the books on the table. "Are all the copies you own of my books this battered?"

"You know what?" With a hollow-sounding slap, Jackson picked up a pristine copy of *Cosmic Contagion* and signed. "Ellie? No surprises in the spelling?"

"Huh? No, I… I can't…"

"It's nothing." He gave Zack a nod and a nudge. "A thank you for sitting with my friend."

"Page 248…"

"Don't!" Jackson snapped at Zack.

"Cost for printing a hardcover book is less than $10," Zack continued, eyes utterly glued to the book. "Is that what her time is worth? I would wager it's worth more."

"Saving my sanity during the signing…" Jackson was now gritting his teeth. "Priceless."

Abruptly, Zack stood with the book and said, "Excuse me."

Another card appeared in Jackson's hand as soon as Zack was out of earshot, and he scrawled a number on the back. "Call him. Seriously. Or text. Whatever. He's super nice but…"

"I…?" Ellie couldn't wrap her mind around what was happening.

"If it leads to a date, that's great. But really… he's too shy to ask."

Carlos' mocking replayed in her head. Would Jackson think the same things? That she'd just used Zack to get into the signing?

And it wouldn't be right to go on a date just because she couldn't refuse Zack's extra signing ticket.

Ellie gulped down the lump in her throat. "I don't want to hurt... his feelings?"

"Is that a question?" Jackson's crooked smile almost made Ellie melt. In other situations, he'd be the kind of guy to steal her heart. "Look. Not my place. But I've known Zack a long time. Did he approach you?"

"Yes."

"It takes a lot for him to talk to someone he doesn't know. But I'm not trying to push. It was lovely meeting you, Master cosplayer Ellie."

Ellie's heart stopped. "How...?"

"Zack's been sitting up here for a half hour while I sign. He found photos from the booths you worked in the past. You know, when he wasn't complaining about my book. Is this yours? Or... rather, mine? Whoa! Is this...?" Jackson flipped the copy of *Zombie Wasteland* around where she'd covered the pages using paint pens, disregarding the original cover art.

Now, Ellie's brain glitched, too. "No! Yes. I mean..."

"These are incredible." Jackson flipped through the ruins of his own book.

"The images are congruent with events on the page." Zack had returned and sat, the pages left to read in *Cosmic Contagion* dwindling.

"Huh..." Jackson kept flipping, every so often squinting at the page and its barely legible text, then nodding. "You're right."

"I usually am."

From the side of the folding table, Jackson's manager tapped to gain his attention. "Pardon me," Jackson grumbled in Zack's direction. He also mumbled something to his friend before marching off to a quiet corner.

"Uh... thank you." Ellie tried, but Zack seemed entirely engrossed in the last pages of his friend's book, so she turned to leave.

"You're welcome. And please ignore Jackson. He firmly believes that I'm incapable of asking a woman on dates without help. May I ask a question?"

The stark frankness brought a small smile to Ellie. She'd had students like Zack. Communication could be stilted or slow, but then she'd unravel the mystery. It was like a switch was turned on, and the words would flow easily, and Ellie could suddenly get through to them. Their refreshing frankness always warmed her heart (if it didn't also tear her to shreds when they critiqued her art).

"Of course."

"Did I make you uncomfortable? Jackson says that I often make women feel uncomfortable."

"No. Actually, I'm glad you sat with me. Thank you for that."

Seemingly satisfied, Zack nodded and closed the book. "I preferred *Epidemic of the Damned*. And not just because Jackson followed more of my notes."

Zack

The alignment slipped when Zack's phone rang. He heaved his shoulders up and held them, then answered. "Jackson."

"So, any news?"

"I'm not sure what you mean."

"What are you doing?"

"Trying to get a better look at Jupiter."

Zack connected the dots before Jackson said, "No interesting phone calls or texts?"

He bit his lip before he said something Jackson would later tell him was regrettable. Even though Jackson was somewhat complacent about doing the same to Zack. "What did you do?" He realized what Jackson did.

"Well, you're stargazing." There was an irrepressible giggle in Jackson's voice. "Thought maybe there was someone special with you or..."

"I can ask a woman out on my own," Zack said, abandoning his adjustments for the time being. "Ellie did not seem interested. So I did not pursue her."

"Oh, she was interested."

"She," Zack pulled at his shirt, tugging it down tight and letting it rebound before continuing, "hung on your every word."

"She watched you. A lot, Zack. And smiled. Come on, she's not even my type."

"According to my observations, your type is a woman. There have not been consistencies in hairstyle, color, body type..."

Jackson laughed. "Sure. You know my type so well, Zack. Ellie did not pay that much attention to me, Zack. You were her knight in shining armor — metaphorically speaking — with the ticket."

An itchiness crept over Zack's body, and he knew why. It always happened when there was too much attention on him.

"Zack, there were four women in the audience. Two did *not* want to be there based on the faces they made while I read. Ellie, though? She seems sweet, and she likes you. And she likes Mighty Con, clearly. So, she's probably a nerd and..."

That assertion, Ellie paying attention to Zack, did not seem to fit with any evidence in the past. Unlocking his screen, Zack returned to the last app open. His socials were still loaded on Ellie's public profile. She was tagged in the pictures from the Mighty Con official booth in an ivy-covered cosplay, more vines than clothing. Her makeup was on point, and her bright red wig curled perfectly.

He tried to turn his attention back to the telescope.

"Bud? I'm proud of you for going for it after the whole Jessica thing. Why did you approach Ellie? Did you recognize her?"

Jupiter taunted Zack through the lens of his telescope. The gas giant beamed down on him with reflected light. "No," Zack admitted quietly. He'd approached her because... well, he didn't know why. Ellie was pretty. And upset. "It doesn't matter."

"You're just going to ignore data? That's not like you. I can give you some data," Jackson's voice turned up like he was getting excited. "Ellie..."

"Thank you for trying, but the statistics are not on my side, Jackson. I would have a greater likelihood of finding Jupiter while you shake my telescope than..."

A text from an unknown number dropped down on the call, but the preview showed: *Hi! This is Ellie...*

"Huh," Zack said distractedly.

"I guess that answers that question. Call me later. Or text me. I want details! And thank her!"

Ellie

The words on the page ran in and out of focus with Ellie's mind. She'd all but assumed she'd have to wait for the library to get a copy of *Cosmic Contagion* or hope she received a copy for her birthday. But here she was, lying on her couch with her annoyingly large gray and white cat she'd adopted, Block, on her chest.

She kept flipping the book closed and reading the name and number on the card Jackson handed her. Zack Hayes.

In her world, between teaching and working at the art store at night, there wasn't time to date until summer break. If the last two summers were any indication, she'd maybe meet a decent guy (not at Mighty Con) and get about two dates in before making the awkward mistake of sleeping with the guy and finding out he had a girlfriend all along. Or a wife. Or, her personal favorite, the inner asshole, became the outer asshole.

Before she knew what was happening, *Cosmic Contagion* lay open on her chest, still in the first chapter, and Ellie was texting Zack.

She'd gone over the words hundreds of times, her thumb hovering dangerously over send before she'd retype the text, hopping between asking Zack on a date and not. Stupid that those words from Jackson FREAKING Wolfe stuck in her head. She settled on something simple. An introduction. Again. And trying not to sound utterly stupid.

> **Ellie:** Hi! This is Ellie from the book signing tonight. Jackson gave me your number. Block's fat tail swished across her legs, depositing the maximum amount of fur possible while she impatiently waited.

What if Jackson had given her a different number? Like Jackson swapped his number for Zack's? Or a number to some random guy across town?

> **Zack:** Jackson told me as much.

God, Ellie read the text ten times. What could she say to that other than clearly, she was talking to Zack?

> **Zack:** He also said I should thank you again, but I'm still trying to figure out what I am supposed to thank you for.

> **Ellie:** I think just for sitting with you.

> **Zack:** But I did you a favor by giving you the ticket. And sat with you after you chose a seat.

Ellie felt the involuntary roll of her eyes and a smile form on her face.

> **Ellie:** Thank you for the ticket. And sitting with me.

> **Zack:** You're welcome.

Ellie considered what she could talk about with a guy she didn't really know. She took the card and flipped it around in her hand again, remembering that Jackson mentioned her cosplay. Zack remembered her from the Mighty Con program, but maybe he also saw her.

> **Ellie:** Did we meet at the con? Have you seen me cosplay?

Goodness, she sounded so dumb. Guys always recognized her. Especially when Mighty Con's advertisements went out, Ellie would usually be smack dab in the middle of several posters. Somehow, guys always saw through the makeup. Astonishing since she could wear full makeup and men would complain about the 'no makeup look' she'd been going for.

> **Zack:** No, we didn't meet. But I remember seeing you at the front of the con.

Ellie felt her cheeks grow red hot. At the front of the con, she'd have been surrounded by people wanting to take pictures. Usually, guys flocked there, sometimes kids, but not as often. It's why she wore so much makeup, so her students' families hopefully didn't recognize her much. Not that being the art teacher meant they cared; it wasn't like she was a homeroom teacher and under as much scrutiny as them.

> **Zack:** Jackson keeps saying I should ask you on a date.

Waiting for a breath, Ellie started typing when another text came through.

> **Zack:** Would you be interested in going on a date?

Ellie stared at the phone, waiting for a response to form in her mind. She kicked herself because why wouldn't she answer yes? By now, most men attending Mighty Con were scared off. But then again, why would a guy who worked in a lab go out with Ellie? She wasn't smart or anything like that. She worked two — sometimes three — jobs to barely make ends meet. Ellie was no one.

> **Zack:** It's alright to say no.

Ellie's heart raced. Zack had a hundred times more courage than she did.

> **Ellie:** Yes, let's go out.

Saturday 10:03 am

> **Ellie:** I wouldn't think you could see much with the lights of the city.

> **Zack:** If the city were any larger, it would be harder. I have a decent telescope for viewing, but I plan to head out to the foothills in two weeks. Jupiter will be in optimal viewing, and my new lens should arrive by then.

Zack: I'm sorry.

10:25 am

Zack: Jackson always reminds me not to info-dump my interests. Especially star gazing.

An image filled with purples and pinks amid a black star field comes through.

Zack: What is that?

Ellie: It's a painting I made. It looks like space, but that wasn't my intention.

Ellie: What if I want to hear more about your star gazing?

Zack: I should ask you about your hobbies.

Ellie: My hobbies can wait. Tell me more about star gazing first.

A compilation of recent pictures Zack saved from various worldwide space agencies sat in a folder on his phone. He chose one filled with swirls of purple and pink and sent it to Ellie.

Zack: A composite of the Eagle Nebula.

> **Ellie:** Why would it need to be a composite? I thought there were super high-powered telescopes.

> **Zack:** There are. But this image combines infrared, X-ray, and optical data from various telescopes to create this high-resolution image.

Would Ellie find it boring? Jackson always said... he tried to ignore Jackson's voice in his head.

> **Ellie:** Huh.

Bingo. Boring.

11:15 am

> **Ellie:** So it's like the layers of a painting?

> **Zack:** Yes.

> **Ellie:** An artist totally looked at those images and decided they needed to go together.

> **Zack:** I'm not sure.

> **Ellie:** It looks like it's glowing. I always love that effect.

> **Ellie:** OMG

Zack: What?

Ellie: I have a freaking brilliant idea!

Chapter Four

A text deluge

Zack

The sterilizer had another four minutes before the cycle would complete. Zack could respond to approximately three email requests in that time, then allow the sterilizer to cool while he had lunch with Jackson.

Or rather, ate the lunch he brought with him wherever Jackson decided within Zack's prescribed four-block radius around the lab.

Priority requests were the majority of the emails in Zack's inbox. The most urgent an amniocentesis on the next truck, which was scheduled to arrive at 12:30 pm. His phone vibrated, interrupting email number 2, a response to a doctor at the closest hospital.

> *Ellie:* I'm not sure which snowman I prefer, but I think I'll be dreaming about snowmen becoming zombies at this point.

Two pictures came with the text. One with pages of similar yet incredibly different construction paper snowman creations, some more abstract than others (eyes where the nose should be and vice versa, or completely deconstructed snowmen). The second picture had five of the same painting of a snowman in a snowy scene.

> **Zack:** I don't understand why you will dream of zombie snowmen.

> **Ellie:** Oops, the third picture didn't send.

Another picture text popped up. Her new copy of *Cosmic Contagion* was splayed open on top of a sketchbook at a rather bland desk, the edge of some construction paper snowmen in the corner. Ellie had dutifully recreated the spaceship with astounding accuracy from Jackson's text.

Someone knocked on the edge of Zack's desk. Bailey, his coworker, smiled shyly. "Your friend is here for lunch. And starting to worry about you."

"He's never late. Why are you late, Zack?" Jackson nervously drummed the doorframe of the shared office space.

Bailey gave Jackson a healthy dose of side-eye and took her seat. "Zack's been answering texts between tests all morning." Turning back to Zack, Bailey snickered, "Your BFF is about to have a full-on panic attack."

"He's what?" Jackson went off the rails. "Are you getting texts from whom I think you should be getting texts from?"

Zack patiently grabbed his lunch bag from the mini fridge that lived between Bailey and his desks, then answered Ellie again while he waited for Jackson to catch up.

> **Zack:** Data suggests that images that sit in the unconscious manifest in less lucid times.

> **Ellie:** What does that mean?

> **Zack:** Maybe if you draw or paint the image in your head, it won't haunt your dreams. Zombie snowmen may chase you down otherwise.

"NO!" Jackson gasped.

"Ellie," Bailey provided, tapping the down arrow rhythmically.

"Did you tell your coworker before me? Because you did not provide me with details. Like any details. All weekend! I asked!" Jackson narrowed his eyes at Zack. "You promised me details."

He'd made no such promise.

"Bailey and I work together. She was sitting next to me when I got a text this morning. And you always say it's rude to keep people on read without responding. I was trying not to be rude."

"It's rude not to tell your best friend when you are chatting with a woman when you promised you would!" Jackson's panic mode was in full swing. Complete with exasperating, deafening exclamations. "Quick, when was the last time you had an actual conversation with a woman?"

Bailey's tattooed arm rose, and Jackson shot her back down with, "You don't count."

"I will eat lunch here if you don't stop blocking the door. There's a time-sensitive test I need to perform in 34 minutes. Your radius of potential lunch venues is dwindling."

Coming right into Zack's uncomfortable space, Jackson laid his hands on Zack's shoulders. "Did you work up the courage to ask her?"

"You said I should ask her on a date." Zack stood and made for the door. "I'm hungry."

"I didn't think you'd actually *listen* to me! What did she *say*?" Jackson said, blocking the way again.

> **Ellie:** Don't want any errant nightmares. Especially any worse than I already have. (shudders) rent is nightmare enough.

Zack backed away from Jackson and plopped back down in his desk chair, watching while Jackson muttered happily to himself.

> **Zack:** As is Jackson.

"What are you saying? Give me the phone!"

Quickly, Zack clutched his phone protectively against his chest. "Why?"

"To make sure you're not screwing it up. She was a nice girl."

"I'm quite capable of inquiring if I am doing well... and socially acceptable..."

In a surprise attack, Bailey came by with a swat to Jackson's head while she passed behind him. "He's doing fine. You're getting over-protective, my dude."

"I have been there for every girl since high school," Jackson said, making an imaginary dot in the air for each girl Zack attempted to ask out. Bailey rolled her eyes again.

Zack watched his desktop lock screen recognize him and unlock. New emails flowed in. "I did not go on a date until my senior year of high school."

"Pity date from Angelica Cantra," Jackson said, turning Zack to face him. "But the point is..."

"The point is, Zack is an adult." Shoving Jackson out of the way, Bailey took a defensive stance between Zack and Jackson. "And doing just fine without you being his constant and undignified wingman."

"And I've also lost confidence in our ability to eat elsewhere." Zack unrolled the crinkled paper bag.

"And when is this mysterious date with? Wait! Like you asked her on a real date, right? Please tell me you didn't just invite her somewhere like to game night."

Zack ignored the second ridiculous question and focused on the first. "Monday night, 7pm."

"Monday? Monday, huh?"

Bailey smirked and instead of checking her test results, seemed drawn back into the conversation. "How long will it take?" she asked Zack as he scrolled through his email and took a bite from his sandwich.

Jackson ran through the mental gymnastics out loud. "Today is Monday, but..."

A sharp snort from Bailey cut through Jackson's loud gasp. "That was so long for him to figure it out!"

"You have a date? Tonight?"

"I have a date tonight. After Ellie's night job."

Fast breaths took Jackson by surprise. "You... can't go on a date tonight. What does she know about you, Zack? You... you..."

Bailey's eyes rolled back, and she stole Zack's napkins, wadded them up, and threw them. "He doesn't need you doing everything for him. The girl's been texting all day. I think our Zackaroni's got it covered."

CHAPTER FIVE

TRACKING SKILLS OF AN ELDERLY BLOODHOUND

Ellie

Ellie picked up paper plates as she walked among the paint-covered tables. Tabletop easels were now empty, and the studio room quieted enough she could hear the low instrumental music she'd put on. The last patrons from her class milled in the back, shouldering on their jackets and lamenting the recent turn in cold weather.

In her own world, thinking about the snowman she'd just taught, Ellie lamented a few design choices and noted where she would change the design next to better suit the students.

Behind her, a man cleared his throat.

"The paint should be dry soon, but I would lay the canvas flat in the back of your car," she answered automatically.

"I guess the third time's the charm."

Ellie's heart stopped, and she dropped the plates in the garbage. "Jackson W-w-w..." Great. Her brain glitched.

"Do you understand how sleuthy I had to get to find you? There are a lot of cosplayers that work Mighty Con and moonlight as art teachers in some way."

"I... I think it's the other way around." Ellie scrunched her face up and shook her head violently. "What are you doing here?"

"I hear Zack asked you out." Jackson followed her, wringing his hands together.

"Yes," Ellie continued her rounds. She'd have to hurry to clean and prep the tables for the next class. "Is there a problem with me going on a date with Zack?" Holy crap, *Jackson Wolfe can't possibly... no...*

"Well," Jackson cut in front of Ellie. "I mean... Zack's... really special. To me. He's..."

They were stopped at the end of an aisle, the garbage can on the other side of Jackson. "Special?" Ellie let out a long breath, wrangling a tangle of emotions before they exploded. "Seriously?"

The guy might have been cool, even suave with his long eyelashes and charming smile, but he was also about to rub a hole in his pant legs with all the nervous fidgeting he was doing. Then the realization dawned, and he stood taller. "Did he *tell* you?"

Ellie bit her lip so that she'd not say something rude. "I *asked*."

"And?"

"And what? Zack confirmed, yes, he is autistic." Ellie shrugged and tried again to sidestep Jackson.

The dude hovered into her path again like a freaking ghost. "And?"

"And *nothing!*" Ellie pushed past with her stack of paper plates, slamming them into the garbage. God, not this bullshit again! "It's not a death sentence. It's not something for him to be ashamed of, either!"

Jackson stopped her, grabbed Ellie's arm, and turned her to face him again. "It's something *you* need to take into consideration."

"It's really not!"

"There are changes you need to consider. Zack hates certain foods and the texture of a lot of foods, and... in fact, there's an entire list of foods he can't stand the smell of. He rarely eats out because it's so hard for him to find something he will actually eat. And don't get me started on..."

"Oh, my God!" Ellie shoved Jackson off her. "You are so dense!"

"I am not saying he's dreadful. Zack is the way he is. But most people cannot tolerate or accept *who* he is. Like, they say they can for a short time and then get fed up..."

"Charming, Jackson Wolfe..." From slamming the plates into the can, Ellie had dipped her thumb in a glob of red paint, which seemed to make Jackson squeamish, but that's what smocks were for. Or almost any shirt Ellie owned. She wiped the glob onto her apron, though admittedly, it looked like she'd been bleeding profusely.

"I may have made a mistake putting the idea into Zack's head. Look, Ellie, I don't want him to get hurt."

"Jackson!" Ellie caught herself before she told the guy to 'catch a bubble' like she would at school. "I *know*. Zack and I have been talking."

"Talking?"

"We texted *all weekend*. And between classes today. And after school."

"Yes, well, I realize you were texting. He was freaking late for lunch! Do you know how rare that is? I'm not sure he has *ever* been late for anything in thirteen years of friendship." Taken aback, Jackson seemed to have trouble doing the math. "But... wait, you're still going on the date?"

"Yes. That's not crazy. What *is* crazy is how Zack wasn't wrong." And she weaved around Jackson to finish cleaning. "He said you don't trust him to talk with a woman of his own accord. Guess he was right."

She hated confrontation, and what had happened, kicking Carlos' chair at the signing, had been a fluke. Still, Ellie turned to face Jackson again, praying she didn't have tears welling in her eyes. "And I'm disappointed I'm wrong. Because I didn't want to believe that Zack's best friend could have so little faith in him." Damn, her emotions always betrayed her. Frustration turned to tears now. "Our date is our business."

"I'm not..."

"Everything alright, El?" Jenna, who took the rest of Ellie's shift so Ellie could go on her date, walked up with the cart of paints for the next painting class.

"This... gentleman just had a few questions." Ellie hoped that was enough for Jackson to take a hint from.

He nodded, but waited for Jenna to move on her way before finishing. "Would you have accepted a date from Zack if I hadn't pushed him to ask you?"

Ellie stood stoic, arms folded over her apron until Jackson relented and tried in a kinder voice, "Where are you and Zack going on your date?"

"Not sure that's any of your business," Ellie fought back a shudder in her voice. All those pesky emotions again. "I get you're protective, but Zack doesn't need kid gloves. Zack's an adult, and despite your staggeringly low opinion, he can make his own decisions."

The brilliant author, Jackson Wolfe, actually sputtered at her. "All I am saying is..."

"You don't trust Zack to navigate the world of dating."

"I... He..."

"Maybe you can leave before he gets here, and you finish smashing his dignity to shards."

"Hey, uh, El? Everything alright?" Mandy, their bartender, came from the storage room carrying a new case of wine. "Don't you need to get ready for your date?"

Jackson huffed. "Look, just handle Zack with care."

A *ting-ting* sounded behind Jackson, but all Ellie could see was red.

Chapter Six

It Ends in Paint Everywhere If You Don't Keep Your Mouth Shut

Ellie

Zack pushed the door open. The red faded away while Ellie tried to read his face, but she'd not been around him since the book signing. His sweet, round cheeks and large brown eyes were blank. The floppy curls messily covered enough of his face, they hid any other expression.

"Jackson?" Zack asked flatly.

Holding her breath, Ellie made a list of reasons Jackson could be here and explanations of why she'd said what she said. The words ran on repeat in her head. She couldn't hurt Zack's feelings because that was *not* how to start a first date, but what if he read differently into Jackson's intentions? Or hers? She'd done nothing but fawn over the author at the signing. Oh, God, what if he thought she wanted to date Jackson instead of Zack and hadn't really come to her senses or something stupid like that?

The train of thoughts had runaway in her mind.

"Hey... buddy," Jackson squeaked.

"Smooth," Ellie muttered. "Zack, it's not what you think..."

All the most credible, completely factual, and believable stories started with: *It's not what you think...*

"Ellie! We set the scaffold up in back — holy shit, it's Jackson Wolfe," Lindsey, Ellie's manager and owner of Making Spirits Bright, skipped in, then ran into the folding tables with the easels for the students. She landed in a tangle with three easels and a bright blue patch of paint streaking up her arm.

There were too many eyes for Ellie's liking. She held her breath and checked her reflection in the mirrored sign behind Mandy, who, incidentally, was doing more wide-eyed watching than actually putting away the wine she'd carried out.

"I think Bailey won the bet she tried to strong-arm me into." Though his tone was still relatively flat, Ellie heard the hurt. "And Ellie is more evolved on the subject of neurodiversity than you, Jackson."

With hindsight being perfect, Ellie wished she'd had her phone out and recorded Jackson Wolfe's utter mortification and squirming, choking on the words he gritted out, "Bailey's just... so smart!"

"Goodbye, Jackson," Zack said with a sidestep, opening up the path to the door.

"Enjoy your date, buddy. Pal."

Zack returned one more reminder to Jackson, "You're behind on your manuscript."

Apparently, Ellie's better judgment was nowhere to be seen because at the pathetic puppy dog face Jackson was making, she mentioned, "You know... I mean... he could join us for a few minutes. It's not like we'll be alone outside..." In his hand, Zack carried a brown cardboard tube. "Is that it? Oh, umm," the eyes on them were now unbearable, but she needed to at least make minor introductions. "Lindsey, Jenna, and Mandy. Umm, the others are outside..."

"Oh,... really? Are you sure?" Jackson asked in such a delicate manner Ellie could feel him tiptoeing. "What was your mystery... date?"

Wielding the tube like a sword, Zack brought it down on Jackson's shoulder. "Follow me to the dark... alley."

Ellie grabbed her coat and wheeled a cart outside, ignoring Mandy shaking a single-serving wine box that would likely inebriate Ellie sufficiently to make an utter ass of herself but take the edge off the date. She waited until they were in the hallway and said, "Jackson's a worrier, huh?"

"He spent all of our lunch hour obsessing over the fact that I was two minutes late getting out of the office. Then he disappeared. I should have made the leap of where he would go, but this afternoon's tests were important, and I couldn't leave Bailey alone."

"I can hear you!" Jackson called out.

"But you don't seem to be using your listening ears." Making Spirits Bright had only three other employees besides those Ellie left inside. Grayson, Carly, and Tamara, all of whom were covered in speckles of white paint and frozen mid-discussion when Zack opened the back door.

Grayson hooted as he pushed up his black-framed glasses, and Ellie pulled out her teacher glare so hard and fast Grayson snorted at her. He recovered poorly, with, "You must be Zack. And... you..." Grayson pointed at Jackson trailing them, "...are familiar."

"We're not going through this again." Ellie made the fastest yet most pain-inducing introductions. They came complete with gasping and an inordinate amount of gaping at Jackson while Zack unrolled a poster. "Wow, this is incredible."

Zack started drawing with his finger. "You could make a grid system."

"Ellie loves starting up top and working her way down. Quadrants are the best you'll get with her if you want a 'grid.' We're in this quadrant down here still making stars." Grayson circled his hand around the bottom left of the poster, mostly a star field.

"So," Jackson bounced around on his feet. "This is the date?"

Zack's level gaze swept over his friend. "We're painting. Well, Ellie is painting, and I brought a poster of the latest combine for star cluster NGC-346, spiral galaxies NGC 1672, and Messier 74..."

"Ok, I get it... kind of."

After a moment of hesitation, Zack finished, "And the 'Pillars of Creation.'"

"Zack loves the stars," Ellie added, a wry smile gracing her face finally.

"Where's the wine?" Jackson joked and leveled his gaze at Zack's slightly raised eyebrows.

"No wine, unfortunately." Ellie studied the poster. "I have to be up early for work."

Digging the proverbial palette knife under her skin, Jackson asked, "Why a space... nebula thing? I mean... ok, that was stupid. There's the obvious..."

"Lindsey wanted to stick it to the antique store that complains about our music when no one is at their store, and it's closed after they kept calling the cops on us for noise violations." The layers of colors were incredible. She studied the high-res photo, removing layer by layer in her mind. Ellie selected a blue color and climbed. "And I'm going to make this baby glow like the freaking sun. Day or night!"

Patting Jackson on the shoulder, Zack gave him a strained smile. "If you don't mind, I'm going up there with Ellie for our date."

Ellie overheard Zack but retreated up the ladder without a word. She played with the colors, mixing and praying that in the poor light it would be good enough to create definition. Not too light or too dark. "I need a sponge!" Ellie called, and three sponges from three angles hit her back.

"Yeah, no..." From the corner of her eye, Ellie watched Jackson back away, waving at Zack. "I'm sorry, Zack. I just... I worry about you."

"I understand the reasoning. But Ellie is correct. Just because I'm autistic does not mean I can't form my own relationships. I've worked hard..."

Jackson had stopped the backward movement. Ellie hung her hand over the edge of the scaffolding, paint dripping from the sponge while she listened. "I know you have. Bud, we've been together forever. I just feel guilty. Like I pushed you into something you're not ready for."

One sponge Ellie loaded with white paint, and aimed...

But Jackson held up his hand and said, "Paint bomb not needed, Ellie. No worries! Right?"

Zack climbed the scaffold ladder and turned to sit with Ellie, their feet dangling and hitting the black painted bricks as their breath made frosty clouds in the frigid air. "No need to defend me further." Zack added, "I appreciate the offer," as if he remembered something else.

Eyes were still on them, but Ellie felt them recede into the night and in and out of the shop.

"I made that drawing you said I should make." Her small travel sketchbook fit in the pocket of every coat she owned. Ellie held it and squeezed, debating if it was worth pulling out. For the first time, at least that she saw, Zack smiled. It happened quickly and could have easily been missed.

"I had a teacher in grade school who would tell me to close my eyes and think of somewhere else I'd want to be when the anxiety got too bad." He unrolled the poster again. "I never found a place here. But I always enjoyed the solitude of staring at a faraway star or artist renderings of nebulas and planets. But now that technology has caught up, we see these places in stunning detail... I am confused. Why are you making that face?"

Shoulders slumping, Ellie sighed. "Don't say artist renderings aren't good enough." She heard that plenty from people all her life. Until they wanted to learn to paint at a place like Making Spirits Bright.

"Artists filled in the gap." He shrugged. "An artist rendering and the new Webb combined images using X-ray, infrared, and optical data is not comparable." Zack seemed to fidget as well. "I'm sorry. I didn't mean to offend you. And..." he pointed at her sketchbook, "... you don't have to show it to me. But I understand. I loathed showing my teachers my creative work. I'd ask them not to read it out loud."

Ellie pulled the sketchbook out; a thick rubber band held the book shut. When removed, the book popped open as the pages curled. Her sketchbook fell open to the last page she'd painted, her zombie snowman.

She sighed, reached down, and patted the thin blue paint into the black, forming the basic shape of the long string of nonsense the internet told her mainly was referred to as the Eagle Nebula. "What do you go to Mighty Con for? Any particular fandom?"

Chapter Seven

Two Dates in a Week Equals What?

Zack

"Dad's birthday is tomorrow. Remember, we're having Uncle Steve and his family over." Zack's mom patted his shoulder on her way by in the kitchen. His mom's hair had lightened more, highlighted by new gray hair. The signs of aging made his chest hurt.

Standing at the stove, Zack worked hard not to think about things he could not control, like the passing of time. Instead, he watched the potatoes boiling, foam forming along the top that he'd occasionally skim off. The Hayes family kitchen always felt warm from the oven constantly being on. But there was something additionally comforting from seeing the aging photo magnets of Zack and his brothers and sisters on the fridge. Zack wasn't the oldest; he had two older brothers, but there were four more under him, the youngest being his sister Casey, who was currently in her princess phase. She wore nothing but princess tiaras and fluffy dresses to school, which his mom assured him everyone thought was 'stinking cute.'

A text interrupted his skimming process.

Noah, towering over Zack, mussed with Zack's floppy curls. They shared their mother's curly dark blonde hair, but Noah kept his hair shorter and what he called more stylish and not 'the same hairstyle Zack had had since he was eight.' "What has my great little bro been up to this week."

"I don't think Mom will be interested in the new Hematology Analyzer our office received this week." Noah always led with a sharp barb, intended to hurt Zack's ego. He was smart, and he always had been, but Zack wasn't a genius or anything. He preferred certain words and science because they made sense. Words followed logic people rarely followed.

"Because, dude, you're not the same species as us. No one is excited about a new analyzer. You were adopted..."

Another text came through. The ramifications of reading the text weighed on Zack. Finally, after skimming what likely was the last of the foam off the potatoes, Zack said, "Mom will be interested in the two dates I went on." Usually, Zack wouldn't say something solely for the reaction, but sometimes (like now), it felt great. And it would change the subject.

"Never the same girl twice," Noah laughed, and Zack realized his mistake.

Information like he'd been on a date or two would be fodder for new teasing.

"Hush, Noah! I'm always excited to hear what is going on in your lab," was what his mom said, but Zack saw the excitement in her eyes. It was practiced control. She kept the giddiness at bay. "Tell me about the Hematology whatchamacallit."

A third text vibrated loudly and didn't go unnoticed by his mom. "Noah, out."

"We're all going to hear the gossip one way or another." His mom made a kitchen towel whip out, catching Noah in the back and chasing him from the room.

His mom's eyes roved over Zack while he finished his dinner task. "What is it? Do you not like this girl? How did you meet her?"

Zack pulled out his phone and checked the messages. "I like her a lot. Ellie came to Jackson's book event last week and didn't have a ticket."

"So," his mom drew out the word until Zack's thoughts came together. "What is the problem, love?"

There were a lot of things now circling his mind. First and foremost were Noah and his comments. But as he scrolled through the messages without reading them, Zack felt the weight of his mom's perception of him.

And all the expectations that came with social obligations.

Zack inhaled and locked his phone, staring at his reflection on the black screen. "I don't want my worth to be based on if I can form a romantic relationship. That's not..."

"It's never been what's most important to you. I know. I didn't want you to think that's the only thing I care about. You love work. And if you would rather tell me about the new machine, that's what I want to hear about."

More sat under the surface. Mom's always seemed to have more, if his and Jackson's mothers were any indication. It exhausted Zack, navigating even the social interactions with his mom.

And then she continued with, "I will say, as a mom... I always worried about you being alone, not in the romantic sense, but just friends. You have Jackson, of course, but I'm not sure who else you have anymore. However, I know you are happy. Whether or not you date this woman, it doesn't matter so much as your happiness, sweetie. That's what matters most to me."

He'd let the texts sit too long. Jackson's words about responding promptly bit him in the ear. One text was a picture of the painting he'd helped her start on the side of the Making Spirits Bright. But now the Eagle Nebula had ships flying from it, from all the biggest sci-fi franchises. While looking at the first picture of the painting, another picture came through, showing off the painting at night with newly installed black lights. The painting glowed red and light purple. "Ellie's an artist."

"Is she?"

"And a teacher. But she hates she doesn't make her own art very much. I think she wishes she could do more."

"And where did you two go out?" His mom tried to busy herself with dinner, though realistically, little was left to be done. The meatloaf was cooking in the oven, the salad had already been prepared, and the potatoes needed more time to boil.

"Our first date was at Making Spirits Bright. I helped her with the mural."

"You did?"

"The reference was a combined image of the Eagle Nebula from the Webb, Hubble — it doesn't matter."

"Sure it does, love. Why isn't it important?"

Zack latched onto details. It was all he could do to keep himself together. "Because as the resolution of these telescopes improves, we see details never seen. And it's... incredible. And those are the details that make a rendering like..." Ellie's recreation wasn't perfect — which she'd warned him would be the case — but he saw the Eagle Nebula. Her understanding of color theory led to neon-like stars practically bursting from the wall during the daytime. They were incredible, and he wanted to walk downtown to see the mural himself.

"What about your second date? Two in one week is fantastic."

"I took her to the planetarium. There was a new eclipse exhibit."

A rare giggle, not the fully bodied laugh but a giggle, escaped his mom. "She makes you smile."

Was he smiling?

"That's rare. And good." His mom rubbed his shoulder, stealing his attention from his phone, and pulled Zack into a hug. When she let go, she said, "Now, if you like, invite her to dinner tomorrow. Not because you have to or because it would be socially acceptable to whomever cares about that garbage, but if *you* want to. We'd love to meet her. Do you want to tell me about work now?"

"You realize your mom saying that means you have to invite Ellie to your dad's birthday dinner?"

Maybe Zack could find Bailey's cell phone number. A diverse field of experience to gather advice from would be better. After what had happened on Monday, Zack couldn't be sure Jackson's advice would be worth asking. But it was better than Noah's, who was the only other person he might have considered asking other than Bailey.

Unfortunately, he didn't have Bailey's phone number in his contacts list.

A more pressing matter escaped Jackson. "What if Ellie gets mad that you don't invite her?"

CHAPTER EIGHT

THE BURDEN OF SOCIETAL NORMS

Zack

His mom's question ate at Zack's thoughts. Paired with Jackson's fervent insistence that Ellie might get angry... or his mom. Why had he asked Jackson at all?

It had already been an anxiety-induced mess when, at dinner, sweat pooled in his palms. Jackson's advice kept Zack's heart rate elevated the rest of the night, especially when he thought about sending Ellie a text and asking her to join him for his dad's birthday dinner. Incoherent dreams haunted him, too. Zack woke Sunday morning and realized the hours left he could ask Ellie were dwindling.

Zack waited at the door of Making Spirits Bright. When he showed up, Zack didn't know when Ellie would arrive. Since it was Sunday, Zack checked the class schedule and realized after waiting for ten minutes that there were plenty of other teachers who could have been scheduled to teach the morning class. He should have just texted Ellie, but every time he thought to do that, sweat broke out again.

Mandy, the bartender, shook out her short, colorful curls and cracked the door open to invite Zack in. She didn't even need to check the schedule. "She'll be here. Lindsey teaches the second class today. El is scheduled for the first class."

Over the years, navigating society, Zack learned enough from trial and error that meaningful conversations were not appropriate over the phone or text (there were a few exceptions, and he was still navigating those... when they annoyingly cropped up).

Ten minutes before the class was supposed to start, people were filing in and taking seats, but Ellie was nowhere to be found. What would the ramifications be if he texted Ellie the question instead?

"Zack? What are you doing here?" Ellie came from the back, tying on a black paint-stained apron.

He jumped and asked, "May we talk?"

"Uh, yeah, Lindsey can start the class." Ellie waved back to Mandy and Lindsey standing at the storage room door, watching with concern.

Making Spirits Bright contained only a few places for a conversation away from prying ears. Leading him back towards the alley, Lindsey and Mandy dispersed towards the main room. Ellie tossed open a small door and ducked in before they hit the alley. "What's up? Is everything alright?"

Zack was flustered at the attention everyone gave him in the last few minutes, and he gripped the ends of his coat sleeves. "My father's birthday is today."

"Ok?"

"My mother invited you, and I am trying not to bend to all the societal pressures of being 'normal', but since she extended the invitation, I've been trying to figure out how best to ask you because Jackson said... well, it might be important to my mom. Although, then

I realized asking you would be bending to those societal pressures, and now…"

"I need to catch up," Ellie said, bringing Zack to the small lunch table. Zack needed to analyze something. The room. Someone possibly designed it as a small office, but the owner of Making Spirits Bright transformed it into a lunchroom. "What is normal?" Ellie asked. "Oh… wait. Is it family pressure? Like questions about if you're seeing someone, if you go out on dates, why you don't get yourself out there more? That kind of thing?"

"Exactly. While my family — no, my parents and my sister — are rather accepting of me as I am, at family functions, I get overwhelmed with the comments from extended family and… some of my siblings. Most of the comments and questions are about why I'm not… normal. Dating and going out with friends. It's why I prefer the museum or going out to the foothills, staring into space, as they would say."

Ellie took in a long breath and reached out for both his hands. "Deep breath, Zack. With me?"

"I'm not sure I'm ready to bring someone to a family function. The attention…" Panic rose again, burning in his chest.

"… will be a lot?" Ellie grinned. "Zack? We've been on two dates. I'm not sure *I'm* ready to meet your family. But I thought about Jackson's question. From the night of our first date. Would I have dated you if he hadn't pushed us to do it? And I figured out the answer." More panic. This had truly been a mistake. He made a mental note not to listen to Jackson's advice any longer. "I probably wouldn't have gone out with you unless you had shown an interest. And I think I would have missed any of the clues that you were interested in me."

"Jackson said you were paying a lot of attention to me." Irrefutable evidence Jackson did not know what he was talking about. Zack tried pulling away, but Ellie kept hold of his hands.

"Did he?" Ellie gave his hands a squeeze, making Zack look up and see her smile, which relieved some pressure in his chest. "Either way, I'm glad we went on our dates. I really like you."

He couldn't keep eye contact with her, his gaze drifted to their hands. "I worry you'll misunderstand my intentions or how I act or respond..."

She squeezed again. "So, you like me too?"

Zack nodded. "Very much."

Another thing still bugged Zack. "But I didn't want to make you angry by not inviting you to my father's dinner."

"Well, I'm not angry. And I wouldn't have been because, like I said... we've only been on two dates." Her thumb bumped along his knuckles in a soothing rhythm. "I'm going to be up early tomorrow for school, but maybe we could go on a date night tonight? I could pick you up after dinner. Your choice! Anything you want to do tonight."

"Jackson says I shouldn't always choose our activities."

"Not terrible advice, all things considered. But you'll have been with family all afternoon and will need an outlet. What do *you* want to do that will help you recalibrate?"

He did many things to decompress or feel more at ease after being around people. Typically, those activities were alone in the confines of his apartment. There was something he enjoyed most... but it was unlikely to be something Ellie would enjoy. Jackson would say it wasn't a typical "date" activity.

CHAPTER NINE

I CAME FOR THE FIRE AND IT DID NOT DISAPPOINT

Zack

"Mom said you were bringing a date," Noah chimed from the hallway, struggling to hold little Casey like a sack slung over his shoulder and somehow still cornering Zack at the front door.

Worse still. Zack hadn't even made it to taking off his jacket. "Ellie is working."

"Suuuuuuuure she is," Noah turned and gave a snort. Casey, in her floofy pink princess dress, kicked and grunted at Noah. His brother stomped up the hallway and yelled, "Dragon kidnapping a princess *coming through!*"

The living room and dining room were full of aunts and uncles, cousins, and more cousins. And Jackson, who latched onto Zack's shoulders. Jackson wasn't supposed to be here.

Zack, exasperated, asked, "What are you doing here?"

Jackson waited, leading Zack through the rooms towards a quiet corner. Usually, the kitchen was the quietest part of the first floor.

Jackson stopped them in a corner of the back room near the entrance to the kitchen, where the noise was dampened enough. Jackson answered, "Your mom was very excited about the prospect of you bringing Ellie. She told my mom, who is up in arms about this."

Zack tried to shrug free and failed. "That does not answer my question. You already know Ellie and insisted I ask her to come today."

"I do, and yes, I did, but I came for the potential fireworks. My mom also heard Noah's been on a rampage, apparently. So, where is she?"

Quietly, Zack peeled his friend's hands off his shoulders, and Zack ducked into the kitchen as soon as Aunt Carol saw him and Jackson in the corner, beamed at him, and failed to conceal a high-pitched squeal. The questions were coming. Well-meaning but overwhelming questions.

The kitchen was no help either; his mom and Aunt Mary were finishing dinner. Great heaping mounds of food lined the kitchen island in disposable aluminum foil trays. There would still be questions here in the kitchen, but without everyone else's attention from the living and dining room would give him.

"Zack, baby! Hey!" His mom unloaded another tray, this time lasagna, on the end of the food train. "Where's your... friend?"

Turning, Zack was utterly alone. Abandoned was the better word. Though it was possible Jackson sacrificed himself to Aunt Carol's unending questions. "Jackson is in the living room. I presume talking about the launch of his new book."

Aunt Mary, her strawberry blonde hair up in a messy bun, grinned at him in a goofy way. Excitement boiled inside, just under the surface. "Your girlfriend," Aunt Mary chuckled and waggled her shoulders.

"Mom," Zack droned and considered leaving now.

"It wasn't me." His mom held her hands up in self-defense. "But I thought you would have asked her to come with how you looked yesterday." Her eyes furrowed with concern.

"I... don't want the attention, Mom. Also, she said two dates wasn't enough time to meet my family, and I agree. It would have been uncomfortable." However, this was ticking all the uncomfortable boxes as well.

"Your mother is just excited. We all are," Aunt Mary said, and he knew she was trying to be helpful, but the pressure kept mounting on Zack. "You've never had a girlfriend."

Unable to bear the questions any longer, Zack gave his mom a tense smile and excused himself.

Somehow, the conversation surrounding Zack and his girlfriend continued. Following him around to whatever room he stepped into. Steering conversations away from a topic was not a strength Zack had. When dinner started, Jackson did what he could, but Noah would interject, "Ask Zack about something real, not some imaginary girl."

Of all his siblings, Casey was the first to stand up for Zack. She came up and waved her scepter around Zack's hair and tapped his head. "I believe you. You're a knight. Knights don't lie."

Kelly, another of his sisters who resembled Aunt Mary more than any of Zack's siblings, slapped a badge on his shirt but whispered, "Better a knight than a dragon, Zack. Ignore Noah, he got dumped and is taking it like a tense little bitch."

"Sarah did not dump me!"

But James, a year younger yet taller and leaner than Zack, added, "Oh, he got dumped big time."

"Dude, Zack has never had a girlfriend. Don't even start..."

James smacked Noah with a dinner roll, earning a glare from their mom as she threatened to make a 'kids table' for everyone under the age of 25 — except Casey, who was not even eating but going around knighting and bestowing lord- and ladyships upon everyone in the family.

But James also said, "No one's sure you have either. Based on the rep I had to fend off when I went to East High, I was better off with being known as Zack's little brother than Noah's. Especially where the ladies were concerned."

The doorbell could barely be heard over the argument between Noah and James, especially when a few uncles and even Zack's father started taking sides and suggesting sports to play to determine a winner, not that Zack knew what his brothers would win.

Casey made a mad break for the door before anyone thought twice.

Ellie

She should have texted again. But she'd sent three texts since Lindsey sent her off after the second class of the day, and no response. Ellie stood at the door of Zack's parent's house; cars lined the street so far she couldn't see her SUV through the light falling snow. Just one more text.

> **Ellie:** I'm not sure if I'm early. Do you want me to come to the door?

Ellie rested her back against the wall. And jumped when the doorbell rang. *Shit!*

Watching herself in the storm's reflection door, Ellie fixed her hair. The door swung open to a small girl dressed in a taffeta and tulle pink princess dress. The little girl's eyes went wide as saucers, and she ripped open the storm door, now staring openly at Ellie's bag. "Miss Elnie! You're Miss Elnie!" The girl ran back off, screaming again into the din of a neighboring room.

Well, double shit. Did this little girl go to the school Ellie taught at?

Waiting at the door, Ellie rechecked her texts. Nothing from Zack.

"It's Miss Elnie! Look!" The girl came back out, dragging someone with her.

"I don't know who Miss Elnie is... oh," Zack lifted the young girl, and she wrapped her arms around his neck. "Ellie?"

"I am sorry," Ellie held up her hands. "I tried texting you, like, a lot, but you didn't answer."

"Whoa... look who the princess dragged in."

"Jackson?" Ellie sighed at Jackson. Damn him. "Are you literally everywhere, following Zack around?"

"Family friend," Jackson grinned again and shoved the last bite of a cupcake into his mouth. "Who is Miss Elnie?" he slurred around the cupcake.

Charming. No wonder people adored this man, and he had women falling all over him.

The adorable girl started pointing and shouting, "She is! Jenna J from ballet said that she was the best art teacher *ever*! She comes and does the coolest art projects! Her projects look like she's learned way cooler things in school!"

"Oh, did she?" Jackson's smile turned devilish.

"Holy crap, the whore of Mighty Con?" Another guy, who definitely bore a resemblance to Zack, lifted a beer to Ellie. "This is your girlfriend? It all makes sense now..."

Ellie sucked in a breath and clenched her fists so tightly her nails cut into her palm.

When the newcomer didn't get a response, he goaded Zack with, "She's super easy and sleeps with guys to get upgrades..."

Unfortunately, this piqued Jackson's interest. "Why did I not know this information?"

"Uh uh!" Ellie felt the irrepressible grip of teaching take over. "We do not talk like that."

"Excuse me?" The new guy, possibly one of Zack's siblings or a cousin, gaped at her.

"We do not talk to our friends like that," Ellie said in the slow, deliberate manner she used in the younger classes. She added a wink at the little girl in Zack's arms. "We should make a good choice. So, what's a good choice here?"

Zack's smile widened, and the girl clinging to him raised her hand up high. "Saying sorry!"

"That's right!" Ellie beamed at the little princess. "We use our kind words, right?" And she leveled her gaze at the guy, waiting.

"Oh, please tell me you talk to Zack like that."

Ellie's voice flattened, "I speak to young children like that when they can't follow expectations." If the absolutely adorable princess was not clinging to Zack, she'd have smacked whoever this was so hard...

"She's a teacher, Noah," Zack responded calmly, searching the coat rack for his jacket. "At an elementary school."

"An art teacher, to be precise. I usually work at Ardmore Elementary, but travel in the district." The girl was making grabby hands for Ellie, but she knew Zack was probably ready to get the hell out of there.

"Jenna J goes to Hoffman!" the princess exclaimed, almost smacking both Zack and Jackson with her hands shooting up to the ceiling.

That explained that...

Noah's smile curled up further. "Now it really makes sense. She's like..."

"Ah ah!" Ellie cut him off. "One, two, three, eyes on me! Last reminder to use our *kind* words."

"I'm not a five-year-old." And Zack's brother gave her an appraising glance, sizing her up in a way that made Ellie reconsider slapping him, even in front of Zack's little sister.

Instead, Ellie kept her gaze steady. "I'll stop treating you like a preschooler when you act like someone older. Because right now, this little one has better manners than you."

"When you came to my friend Jenna J's school, you taught them how to paint fall trees! Jenna J showed me how, and I made six trees!" She held up one hand, fingers spread, and counted them. It took a moment to decide she needed another finger to make six.

"This is my sister, Casey," Zack said while frantically trying to find his jacket one-handed among the pile of coats. "And my brother, Noah."

"We need to back up, Miss *Elnie*?" As if it were right in front of Zack's eyes the entire time, Jackson pulled Zack's coat off the rack.

"Five-year-olds can't always say Eleanor. And at my school, there's another Ellie, Elizabeth Hanley, so... it stuck. The littles like calling me Miss Elnie."

"That's actually surprisingly sweet." Taking Zack's place, Jackson picked up Zack's little sister. "What are you two crazy kids up to tonight?"

"Trying to leave before my entire family moves into the foyer." Zack gave his sister a peck on the cheek. "And the questions get more uncomfortable than they already are."

The little girl arched back in Jackson's grasp to tell Zack, "She's a princess. Knights belong with princesses." Casey shot Noah a death glare to end all little kid death glares. "Dragons don't!"

Giving Casey a wink, Ellie said, "Smart girl."

"Mom!" Noah yelled.

"Let's go," Zack insisted.

"Are you sure? I'm here early. Are you done with dinner?" Ellie worried. "I can come back..."

Noah sang, "You haven't had cake, Zack-y boo."

Jackson tried covering Casey's ears with one hand. "Maybe he'll get some cake," and waggled his eyebrows.

"No cake." Zack actually pushed Ellie through the door gently. "We're going to my apartment and watching Fellowship tonight."

"Seriously?" Noah sighed. "You put up with this geek?"

"Sure. Fellowship is my favorite." Ellie giggled at Zack. Now he had her arm with both hands to better drag her away. "Who knows, we might even chill tonight," Ellie shot both Jackson and Noah a grin over her shoulder, which was made infinitely better when Noah choked on his beer.

"There... is... no... way..."

"It's not the first time I've had sex, Noah," Zack called from the front yard.

Ellie's cheeks heated. Oh, she never should have said anything. Quickly, Ellie waved at Casey, giving her a quick 'shh' and growling back, "Not the thing to say with your *little* sister around!"

"Noah and my oldest brother, Daniel, have said it all around Casey."

Ellie turned Zack towards her SUV. "And apparently, she knows someone who has been in my classroom! This can't get back to a parent!"

They'd climbed into her SUV when his phone buzzed. Zack pulled it out, trying to swipe away the messages he'd missed from Ellie, and opened one from his mom. Ellie really didn't mean to read it over his shoulder, but when she started her car, habit made her turn her head to the right and pray the damn thing would start (a holdover from her first, crappy sedan that was older than her).

> **Mom:** Casey mentioned Ellie stopped by. Have fun on your date with your princess.

> **Mom:** I'm sorry everyone was putting so much pressure on you. Take your time, sweetie. When you both are ready, Ellie is welcome anytime.

"It wasn't too much pressure?" Ellie dared to ask.

A small, kind of tense smile quirked up on his lips. "It was. But maybe if you're there next time..."

"I'd like that." Ellie grinned. "I'll just have to remember to muster my inner teacher ahead of time. For Noah."

"I'd like that, as well."

ESCAPING CHRISTMAS

A NOVELETTE

CHAPTER ONE

Jackson

Thick gray clouds hung low and menacingly. Jackson had thought nothing of it. A little snow was predicted to add to the couple of inches on the ground. The last time Jackson had looked, the Christmas Eve weather report was a dusting. Dusting meant little.

Dusting did *not* mean a thick blanket of unpassable crap falling in a whirlwind. Jackson slammed on the steering wheel of his coup and searched for the road's edges. He could still make it to the airport, or so he kept telling himself. In reality, he could make it to the airport as long as he could find the edges of the street and stay on it without sliding off into a mountainous snowbank. And as long as he did not get hit at the next intersection because there was no way to see the traffic light in this blizzard.

But, honestly, it wasn't a blizzard. Because if it were a blizzard, blizzards mean planes don't take off. And if his plane does not head to Miami in two hours with him on it, Jackson would be stuck at home. With his family.

On freaking Christmas!

That was not about to happen! Christmas day in the Wolfe household amounted to all the drama one could imagine. For the last five years, Jackson would fly out on Christmas Eve to 'prepare' for a yearly science fiction writers' convention in Miami. His mom was always disappointed, but there wasn't the Aunt Cam gossip and the comments that were becoming more than microaggressions as she got older. One year, Jackson had not kept his mouth shut, and Jackson's mom was fielding pissed-off calls from family for months after a wine-induced rant Jackson went on against Aunt Cam.

Miami was a great trade-off. Jackson spends Christmas Eve with his parents, then leaves and does not bring down the entire Wolfe family's house of cards on Christmas Day.

Something hard struck Jackson's car, sending him careening into a bank on what he assumed was the side of the road. He didn't see the light pole until his coup's front end crunched up.

"Come on!" Jackson punched the airbag back down. "What the hell?" He was barely at the edge of town. There was another five miles to the highway and another twenty minutes to the airport. "Merry freaking Christmas." Throwing his shoulder into the door, Jackson got out just as the four-wheel drive SUV drove off, fishtailing a bit as it went. "Really?"

The frigid wind and whipping snow forced Jackson back into his car. He tried 911, and the operator put him in a queue but warned that they were fielding so many calls she could not guarantee when emergency personnel would get to him.

His parents only had sedans and none with four-wheel drive (not that he would call his parents in this ridiculous blizzard to get him).

He drummed on the wheel, feeling the cold seep into the car, and scrolled through his recent texts. Who could come to help him on Christmas freaking Eve?

Zack

"All flights were canceled," Zack scrolled through the news that popped up in his alerts. The weather report was getting worse as the minutes went on since dinner ended. All they were trying to do was get on the road, but there'd been a lot of delays. Ellie, though, was visibly brightening. Whenever Ellie beamed, Zack realized he felt a weight in his chest come up, too.

"It's not snowing that bad," Ellie adjusted her sweater, found her scarf and hat, and then piled them into her thick jacket. "We can make it to my parents..."

"Honey?" Zack's mom entered their ornately decorated front hall, worrying and drying plates at the same time.

Ellie had marveled at the decorations, and his mom made a point of commenting that she must really love Christmas. He still hadn't found a time to actually ask her if she did. This was something a boyfriend should know, given his brother's taunts of 'What kind of a boyfriend are you?' throughout dinner.

His mom wrung her hands. "Are you sure you want to head out? The news just said..."

His phone buzzed, and Zack caught the flag notification. "Jackson just texted," Zack said, then mouthed the words of the text silently.

"Oh dear," his mom muttered. "He didn't make it out in time?"

"What do you mean out?" Ellie asked. "I thought his parents lived next door."

"Jackson has found the holidays run more smoothly when he is not present for them." Then Zack reread the text.

"The airport's closed now since all flights were canceled until the snow lets up." Zack's mom turned to return to the dishes. "There's a story I'll tell you another time. Although, I'm not sure you both will be able to get out of town either. Not with how this snow is falling."

Zack frowned, a ball of panic quickly taking over. "He's stuck in a snowbank."

Whatever worry Zack was feeling, Ellie didn't seem concerned in the slightest. She was out the door, hands on her hips, surveying his parent's street. "Did he call for a tow truck?"

"Tow. Police. Fire Department. He said they're all backed up with accidents and issues from the snowstorm." More worryingly, Jackson wasn't answering his texts anymore.

Ellie tossed Zack his jacket. "Alright. Come on."

"Uh?" Anxiety welled in his chest at the thick blanketing snow falling, joining with the feeling in his stomach. It turned to a burning that was growing by the second. "I'm unsure we will be able to…"

"It's, what, a few inches?" Ellie shook her head and even gave a light laugh.

He'd spent enough time with his family, and Zack was ready to leave and decompress. Hours worth of driving was enough to regulate again before more social… obligations. But he hadn't been expecting the snow. He should have. Obviously, but now, the thought of heading out in the swirling vortex of snow made Zack come close to shutting down. "The city closed the airport."

Ellie's reaction confused him. She shrugged. "It's not like up north."

"You say up north, but you grew up two hours away. That's not 'up north'."

"It is compared to here." Ellie found the shovel by the side of his parents' garage and dug out the end of the driveway. "There's a huge difference in winter weather when you travel two hours north from here. This isn't normal down here. You get maybe an inch or two, and that's a lot. But this isn't that bad."

"Honey?" Zack's mom called behind him, followed by his brother, Noah, mockingly calling out like his mother. "I've got more bad news."

Catching Zack's dubious nose wrinkle, Ellie grinned, stabbed the shovel into the snow piled at the edge of the driveway, up to Ellie's knee, and asked, "What bad news?"

Okay, Zack had misjudged how much snow had fallen. This wasn't a few inches. At least six more inches had fallen and was still coming down heavily.

"The highways are closed. State police are recommending staying off all roads."

The burning feeling radiated to his fingertips now. "Ellie, I think it's best to stay here tonight." Zack joined her in the driveway, clenching and unclenching his fists.

Ellie

Brushing off a few inches of fluffy snow from her SUV's windshield, Ellie checked through the back window to see if there was enough room to hold a third person. Unfortunately, she'd piled paintings in the back for her parents and one for Zack's parents. Three paintings were left, one long enough that it took up the entire back seat. Ellie unlocked the doors and considered how best to remove the paintings. They all should fit on top of her and Zack's overnight bags in the trunk. Before they left Making Spirits Bright, she'd been concerned that the canvases would slip and deform against the bags, so they ended up in her backseat.

Ellie considered her alternatives and whether to check in with her mom. If she called her mom, she'd get an earful if she said they would still drive up in this storm. A short distance in the trunk with their bags would probably be alright, but not all the way up to her parents' place. Ellie shuffled out the top painting around the seat back and through the door, twisting so the frame cleared the odd door shape.

"And leave Jackson in a snowdrift?" She considered the alternatives. "I mean, I'm okay with that, but are you?"

An internal conflict weighed on Zack, so Ellie took the time to carefully bring the painting around to the trunk. Growing up in the northern Midwest didn't mean Ellie was immune to slipping when there was an inch of hard-packed snow on the driveway. She landed with a crack, and a lot of sharp pain shot through her hands.

"Ellie?" Zack carefully shuffled towards her. "Are you hurt?"

"No," Ellie cursed and slammed her hand against the splintered wood of the canvas frame. Maybe her pride was hurt, or was that just straight-up disappointment that she'd stupidly ruined her mom's Christmas gift?

Zack's hands reached under her armpits and helped steady her as she stood back up.

"Damn it!" Somehow it felt like Jackson hovering over her, working to ruin another thing between her and Zack. Not intentionally, but his unintentional blunders were a mounting strain on her and Zack's relationship, no matter how new the relationship was. She saw movement at the open front door. "You really want to stay with Noah?"

Three hours and counting for dinner and exchanging gifts. Zack would easily admit the prospect of leaving was palpable. And he'd been excited, or as enthusiastic, as he could get about the dreadful new experience of meeting Ellie's family.

Zack's older brother, Noah, appeared at the door, still dressed in his dress shirt and jeans, but he had unbuttoned a few of the top buttons and was rolling up his sleeves. "Which family house you two gonna bunk in tonight?"

"Noah Hayes, get your butt in here and help me with the dishes."

"I'll get the chains and put them on my tires if it would make you feel better," Ellie said, as eager to leave as Zack. Especially before she did something she'd regret.

Zack countered with the only fact he knew, "Chains are illegal on wheels now."

"I swear, we'll be fine going out and getting Jackson. I've got four-wheel drive; my dad wouldn't let me move out of the house without a decent SUV. I got this." She kicked the snow and looked up and down the empty street. "I'm going. You can text me where Jackson is, I'll pick him up. I promise to not leave him out to freeze for Christmas. Consider it an extra Christmas gift to you."

Noah made squeaking noises and sauntered down the hallway before he kicked the door shut.

"I'm coming."

"Which argument won?"

"Staying with my family tonight seems the most tortuous of options. Even if we end up in a snowbank as well."

"You'd rather hazard a blizzard than stay here?" Ellie grinned, hoping Zack had caught her sarcasm.

He smiled back and gave a soft shake of his head. "And I don't want Jackson to be left in the cold. But we're not driving north. Right?"

"Promise. We'll figure out where it's safe to stay once we get the idiot who thought he could fly out in this storm."

"Says the woman who wants to drive out of town in this snowstorm."

CHAPTER TWO

Jackson

Jackson zipped his leather jacket to the top and stamped his feet. The inside of his car felt as cold as the blizzard outside. He bounced his dead cell phone on the steering wheel. He'd tried to get more texts off to Zack about a plan or what he could do, but the damn battery decided it was the best time to die!

So preoccupied with getting anywhere away from the icebox his car had turned into, Jackson jumped, knocking the steering wheel, when something knocked on the window. He hadn't seen anyone pass by in over an hour. Flannel and layers of cloth over a thick coat and gloves knocked again. The person, hidden under all the layers, pulled down several scarves. "Jackson!"

"Zack?" Jackson opened the door, crouching behind it to speak without getting a mouthful of snow. "What are you doing here?"

Ellie came around the back of his car. "Did you really try driving in a blizzard in this tin can? That's a little pathetic. No wonder you skidded out."

Chattering, Jackson fired back, "Someone hit me. And drove off. And it's not pathetic. It's my car! It's perfectly fine for our stupid winters, but someone brought their northern snowstorms with her, apparently! How did you get here?"

"Ellie drove. Come on." With all the layers, Zack waddled to a running SUV with Ellie in tow. "All the highways are closed. Airport, too."

"How did you find me? I never got back to you about where I was!" Wrenching his seat back down, Jackson reached for the suitcase in the back.

"Your texts came with location info. You never hide it," Zack said, his voice muffled by the scarf. "Come on. I'm cold."

"Where are we going? Everything's closed. And now you can't get out of town either."

Ellie sighed, brushing snow from her windows with gloved hands. "Probably too late to go back to your parents' place, Zack."

"I'm not sure what options that leaves us with." Zack stomped the snow off his boots onto the carpet, which Jackson watched, absolutely appalled.

"Uh, well," Ellie's eyes bored into Jackson's. There was something there she didn't want to say, but apparently, against her better judgment, she finally said, "I guess we can go to my apartment."

"How far?" Jackson's teeth now chattering so hard he thought he'd crack a tooth.

Ellie stood in the door of the driver's side. She wore warm layers, but not in the overabundance as Zack. "About a block that way."

Jackson climbed in the backseat after a fight with the doorway and his suitcase. "Haven't you been to the little lady's apartment yet?"

Yanking his hat off, Zack shook out his flattened yet still perpetually floppy hair. "I have not."

After a controlled exhale, Ellie said through gritted teeth, "There's a lot of crazy men. I learned my lesson."

"How long do you wait until you bring a guy home?" Jackson asked, interest piqued.

Warming his hands on the heat vents, Zack mentioned, "I was going to her family's house. To meet her parents."

"That's one thing, dude. But you haven't been to her apartment yet? You all have been dating a while."

"She's stayed at my apartment. Five times, to be exact."

"That's not... you're skirting around the question. And I wasn't even asking you, Zack!"

"Girl's gotta stay safe," Ellie growled.

"And you said we'd stay there after we returned from Christmas at your parents."

"You don't have to tell Jackson *that*." The tension in Ellie's shoulders was so tight she seemed ready to snap in two. "Is it really any of your business?"

"Whoa, pipe down, princess. I'm grateful for the ride..."

"And?" she was now holding her breath.

"And concerned about you being able to get anywhere in this insanity. Look, the windshield is already covered again."

Throwing the car into reverse, Ellie backed up without preamble. Jackson scrambled to put his seatbelt on. Then he tapped Zack on the shoulder. "She does know there's a lot of crazy women out there too, right?"

Her SUV didn't fishtail, but she swerved a bit, and Jackson watched her white knuckle grip the steering wheel. "Pretty sure most crazy women you run into don't stalk you to the point of needing to move. Maybe they do... but..."

"Oh..." The ice-cold feeling returned, but with a healthy dose of morbid curiosity.

"I did not feel like moving again."

Leaning forward as far as the seatbelt would allow, Jackson grinned as he got under Ellie's skin again. "I kind of want to hear this story. Is that rude? I'm being rude, right?"

Zack reached for the handhold above his head and held the seat. "If we're trying to keep the night free of anger and you don't want to walk home, I advise against wanting to hear more."

"Did she tell you? Come on, princess. I want to hear it!"

His voice was low — which Zack generally did not have the tact to lower his voice — he whispered, "I gleaned it ended in a restraining order."

"Well, obviously."

"I can literally hear every freaking word you are saying! I will leave you here, Jackson Wolfe. So help me..."

"She's grumpy. Is Ellie grumpy to you?"

Zack chose not to answer the question and instead said, "I never wanted to meet a houseful of new people more in my life than right now."

"Wow, bud. You dread those kinds of meetings." And then it clicked. Maybe Jackson should shut his mouth.

Ellie

Ellie set her headlights to bright and blared through the snow, taking Parker St carefully, making sure to stay between the slowly condensing edges of the street. Signs were a blur of snow-nados caught against the brick facades or half-covered, nearly impossible to read. Except for Dragon Palace, the restaurant she lived above. Mrs. Li must have kept Mr. Li busy, shoveling the sidewalks and brushing off the restaurant sign with a broom every 20 minutes by how pristine the front of the restaurant looked, with its vibrant red neon shining through the storm. But getting into the alley was another story entirely.

The alley was somewhat protected from the storm, but the couple of plow passes made so far blocked the entrance to the alley. Ellie got out, found the shovel sitting against the side of the building, and dug a trench wide enough for her SUV. Zack stayed in the front seat, already back to being bundled to the brim, barely recognizable in all the knit and down jacket layers. On the other hand, Jackson made a menial gesture to try to 'help,' but Ellie rolled her eyes. The guy was in expensive loafers; what the hell did he think he would do in that and his suit, plus a jacket that wouldn't even protect him from a light breeze? It was faster if Ellie shoveled on her own. In a few minutes, her car could pass through into the back alley, which should be good enough to keep her car hidden and safe from the plows.

Zack extricated himself from his seatbelt and turned to stare at the red neon sign. "I'm very confused. Where do you live?"

"Above the Dragon Palace. Mrs. Li rents an apartment against Mr. Li's better judgment." And Mrs. Li was also the queen of gossip. She generally heard when Ellie's biggest asshole ex was roaming around the neighborhood. "Come on, the back entrance has the stairs to the top floor."

Ellie opened the trunk and wanted to do nothing else but cry. Sure, she could easily repaint the stupid mountain cabin scene, but it was the principle. In the most literal sense, it was painful as her hands still stung from the fall, a reminder of what happened to this Christmas. It broke into sharp, bitter pieces. Removing the painting, Ellie released a slow breath through her teeth and carried the broken frame pieces and limp canvas to the door. Juggling that and her keys, Ellie rammed the door with her hip one, two, three times to push past the rusty lock and hinges.

With all the layers, Zack shuffled unsteadily in while Jackson gave Ellie a stupid grin. "What?" Ellie snapped.

"This is so boho artist of you."

"It's so about to be you freezing your ass off in the alley if you don't stop giving me shit." Did she feel bad for snapping? Maybe.

"I miss the naivete of the star-crossed Jackson Wolfe fan."

Maybe not.

"Jackson?" Zack asked after pulling down both scarves he wore. "This would be when you tell me not to keep talking because I am pissing someone off."

"Yes, that is true." Jackson's ever-present grin fractured her calm, and Ellie didn't realize how present it was until now.

She settled into the door and considered what would happen if she swung the broken pieces of canvas frame at Jackson. Some people might call it assault, but if they *knew* Jackson Wolfe, it might be different. "*You* wouldn't understand."

They traipsed up the stairs, Ellie keeping an eagle eye out for Mrs. Li, who always seemed to be around to be in her business at the most inopportune times.

The top floor had three doors in a short, dingy, dimly lit hallway. Ellie's door was instantly recognizable. The second advantage to living above the Li's restaurant. They adored having an artist around and did not care that Ellie transferred paint to pretty much everything she touched, including her front door. That had no number on it. Ellie unlocked her door and then hesitated. "Zack?"

"Yes?" he was still stripping off layers and picking them up to drape across his arm.

"It's going to be... a lot. You know, sensory-wise."

"I'm prepared."

She highly doubted he was prepared. Her entire plan for the holiday had been to prepare Zack all during Christmas. The sensory overload of parties with his family was one thing; he could easily excuse himself from his family. But with her family, he might find it harder to speak up (though likely not because he was so frank with anyone he encountered). The Chapman family alone, as in her immediate family, were a handful. And in that instance, it was just her parents and one brother. Also, her mother had been obsessed with Christmas decorations since before Ellie was born. All the hallways and every flat surface of her childhood home were covered in an array of Christmas items. Visually, it would overload anyone, neurotypical or divergent.

Well, Ellie's apartment was the same. Except filled with art. The small studio she rented from the Li's was cozy, primarily because of all the carts filled with art supplies, easels (which there were no less than three open with projects in various stages of life), sketchbooks, art books, and media of all every sort littered her couch, the small island in the kitchenette and even around her bed. When she'd moved in, the floor was a gorgeous but unmaintained, darker wood floor that Mrs. Li said would have to be refinished later anyway, so if Ellie got paint on it, it wasn't a big deal. And she did. When surfaces weren't covered in art supplies, they were covered in Block's cat fur.

"I hope no one is allergic to cats," Ellie shuffled in and quickly started tidying up. First, the couch, so there was some place to sit, but then she realized her bed was unmade and the kitchen was a mess in the opposite corner.

At this point, Ellie thought her mom would realize she hadn't called to tell her they were on their way up. This meant... cue worried text soon...

Ellie dropped the broken painting on top of the first surface she could (a stool at the kitchenette island) and continued making rounds, grabbing anything she saw and tossing it in a bin or cart wherever there was room. On her way past, Ellie kicked the switch to turn on her 4 ft Christmas tree, decked out in homemade ornaments, this year all paper and made from watercolors. The lights daisy-chained up to the ceiling, vaulting over her at about ten feet (Mr. Li's ladder came in handy to decorate the ceiling). Ellie had painted a mural before she met Zack that was a pitiful comparison to the nebula she painted on the side of Making Spirits Bright. But this one was inlaid with glow-in-the-dark stars, like Ellie had in her room growing up, which, paired with the strung-up lights, made the apartment feel filled with stars.

Jackson whistled. "Definitely an artist. Damn..."

But it was Zack she was worried about. He'd finally made it through all his layers of coats, scarves, etc. He gazed around the room, and Ellie's worry jumped onto her sleeve, metaphorically at least. "So? Zack, I mean... and when the Li's are cooking, it smells like nothing but Chinese food up here, which I mean I don't mind, but..." Ellie was babbling.

"I expected no less. I'm happy you have art. You always seem incredibly sad you don't make your own art."

"Well, that is a lie, isn't it? I mean, look at this?" Jackson flipped through a wood frame on the floor filled with paintings.

"Get out of there!" Ellie dashed across the room to Jackson, but froze before she got to him. Her phone vibrated with a text. "Oh, no."

Zack stared up at the ceiling, his face still blank, hair falling back, better revealing his face. "It's not as good as the other one. I did this one last year, and..." God, her palms were slick and yet sticky, and words would do nothing tumble out of her mouth if she didn't get a handle on it.

"Omega..." Zack's voice trailed off, and it took Jackson passing by and falling onto the only open spot on the couch with a loud clap of his hands to break Zack from his mumbling. "It's like the Omega Nebula, also known as the Swan Nebula. It's in the Sagittarius constellations..."

"Okay, we get it," Jackson sighed.

"Umm," Ellie ignored Jackson and touched Zack's shoulder gently. "I should call my mom. She's worrying; this is only the first of a bazillion texts she will send. Um...?" Why was asking Zack to join her harder than asking him to drive to her parents' place for Christmas?

Oh, right. Jackson's stupid, watchful eagle eye was on them. That's why.

"Just ignore me. Call your mom, introduce your *boyfriend*."

Ellie threw her arms around Zack in a quick hug and then dragged him away from Jackson and into the kitchenette, searching for her tablet along the way.

Placing the call was almost as hard as asking Zack to be on the call with her (even if she didn't actually ask him). Her mom picked up on the third ring, and her mom's scream nearly knocked Ellie off her stool. Her mom's dark brown hair was filling in with silver highlights. She'd been working out more since Ellie left home and was more toned than when Ellie was younger, but she hadn't lost what her mom still called the baby weight (even now, decades later). "You're safe! Daniel! Eleanor is safe! The storm is all over the news!"

"Yeah, mom," Ellie sighed. "If we left earlier..."

"No, no! You stay put. Don't you think of driving up here. You've got too much of your dad in you." Her mom had yet to acknowledge Zack, though he was barely in the frame. "You got home alright, I see.

And what about…?" Ellie turned the tablet and put Zack in the frame. "Oh, honey. Hello! You must be Zack!"

"Hello, Mrs. Chapman." Zack waved once and placed his hand awkwardly in his lap.

"Dude," Jackson whispered harshly behind them. "More."

Zack, distracted by Jackson, pressed his lips together in deep thought. "It's… nice to meet you?"

"Oh, do you have another friend over, love?" Off in the living room, Ellie could hear her dad swear at the Christmas lights that were inevitably burnt out.

"Yeah, um, one of Zack's friends got stuck trying to get to the airport."

"Not the night for that, I'm afraid. Is he trying to get home?" Ellie shook her head stiffly. Her mom's face grew on the screen. "What's the matter, dear?"

"Nothing," Ellie lied. Bold enough, she hoped her mom would gloss over it since Zack was sitting beside her. But there was the sharp pain of the broken frame still shooting through her hand, like the jabs Jackson made at her. All of them were a reminder of a fractured holiday, a first broken holiday Ellie could remember. All she wanted was to be home. Sometimes, since the whole stupid ex-fiasco, that's all she had wished to move home, proverbial tail between her legs.

"Oh dear, that was a terrible lie, Ellie honey," her father appeared, mostly a blur passing behind her mom.

"I just—" *She didn't want to say it in front of freaking Jackson Wolfe!* He would just gain more fodder to use against her in the future. But her mom made *that* face, the one that all moms could make. The one that preceded utter humiliation. "I just haven't missed a Christmas yet."

"And you broke that painting's frame," Zack added for an extra special helping of humiliation. "Is your hand alright?"

"Did Zack say you got hurt?"

Ellie felt her palms start saturating her pants.

"Did you put the chains on your tires, sweetie? I don't get it. Why is she still home?"

"She's not driving up here *during a blizzard,* Daniel!" Her mom chastised her father again in passing.

"It's what... a foot of snow! Psh, that's nothing. You'll be fine, sweetheart, just come on up..."

Her mom beat back her father with a kitchen towel. "Ignore him, sweetie. You stay put. And stay warm. Who's your other friend...?"

"Oh... well..."

"Jackson and I have been friends since elementary school." Zack offered incredibly helpfully.

"It's fine, mom. We've got the couch and the bed and blankets. It will be... fine."

"Eleanor, dear. Calm down. We'll do Christmas in a few days. You can come up this weekend, especially if Zack is off work. I would love to meet him in person. It's just a day. Nothing to worry about."

"It's a day I've never missed with you, Mom."

CHAPTER THREE

Jackson

Well, shit. Ellie hid in the kitchen, initially heating water for the soup she found she didn't have. She actually cursed and flipped off the stove. Her cupboards weren't utterly bare, but there wasn't much in them.

Block, her cat she introduced about ten seconds before Jackson got swiped at, sat, judging Jackson and Zack's worth. Somehow, the damn animal thought Zack worthy and let him pet its head and only its head, whereas Jackson got hissed at.

"Hey, so Ellie seems bummed."

"Astute observation, Jackson." Zack kept giving Block overly gentle pets right in the center of its fluffy white head, then immediately shaking the hair off and repeating.

"How was Christmas at your parents' place? Noah wasn't too much of an ass, right? Did Ellie have fun?"

Zack gave a slight shrug. "I do not think it's the same as seeing her own family."

"Duh!"

His friend's hand hovered over the cat's fuzzy head. "I don't know how to help. Ellie seems miserable."

"Me either, bud." Oh, that's what was eating at Jackson. Guilt. Like he'd done something to ruin Ellie's Christmas. Not that driving through a blizzard for his plane to warmth and sunshine but getting knocked into a snow-covered streetlamp had been on purpose.

"Do you still like Ellie?" The question from Zack smacked Jackson like the car that had hit him earlier.

"What do you mean?" He was not *dumb* enough to hit on his best friend's girlfriend. Had he been flirting? Was his voice freaking cracking right now?

"You made such a big push for us to go out on that first date, but you two always fight. Do you not like Ellie any longer? Is it a mistake for me to keep...?"

"Oh, God! Don't even say that out loud! *You* like Ellie, right?"

Zack's response was immediate. "Yes, a lot."

"Then nothing changes. I think..."

"I think," Ellie interrupted, "I can literally hear every word you say." A distinct sadness tinged her voice. "I don't hate Jackson. I just don't see him as the author I idolized... I mean... admired." She slammed a cabinet so hard that Jackson jumped and checked the wooden door for cracks even from across the studio apartment.

A frantic knock startled Zack and Jackson.

"Who the hell is here?" Jackson pulled up Zack's sleeve and checked his smartwatch. No new texts since he'd dug out his phone charger and got his phone back up and working. "Did her dad drive down here to spite the weatherman?"

"I think that would spite the governor who declared the state of emergency."

"Ellie! Ellie Chapman! I hear voices. You okay?" The voice was strong and as fiery as the hard knocking that continued throughout her talking.

Ellie opened the door to a shorter, elderly woman with silver close-cropped hair and a stoop to her spry step. "Merry Christmas Eve, Mrs. Li. I thought you were keeping the shop open."

"The shop is open! You are not supposed to be here! You were going home!" Apparently, Mrs. Li could be in the dictionary under the word 'fiery.' Ellie backed up a few paces.

"The storm closed everything, Mrs. Li. I can't drive up..."

"Who is that?" she interrupted, jabbing a finger at Zack and Jackson. "Who are you with? What is going on, Miss Ellie? Do I need to get my broom?"

Holding a pillow up as a shield was the only way Jackson could say, "I'm terrified of this little woman getting a broom."

Zack nodded furiously.

"Mrs. Li," Ellie sighed and winced preemptively, "this is Zack, my... boyfriend."

"Mmm, yes." Mrs. Li squinted at Zack. "The hair."

Jackson prodded Zack and then pressed him again to get Zack to say a simple "Hello."

"Who is the other one? Ellie Chapman, you better not be doing anything un... un... what is the word?"

Pulling out the most charming smile in his arsenal, Jackson stood, dropping the pillow back on the couch. "I'm Jackson Wolfe. *The* Jackson Wolfe."

Mrs. Li narrowed her eyes and advanced, stomping harder with each step. "I will get my broom! Do not think for one minute..."

"He's Zack's friend!" Ellie rushed between Mrs. Li and Jackson. "His car got stuck in the snow. He's just staying here for the night."

"Better not be any funny business up here, Eleanor. Come on." Mrs. Li snatched Ellie's hand and dragged her down the hallway to the back stairs. "Come on! I'm not getting any younger."

Before another broom assault was threatened, Jackson herded Zack downstairs, jogging to catch up before they lost Mrs. Li in a labyrinth of curtains, doors, and strange little hallways.

"Sit. Sit." Mrs. Li practically pushed Ellie into a yellowing bench seat. "I'm making soup."

Jackson looked over at Zack, settling in next to Ellie with only a hint of a soft smile that was so uncharacteristic for him. Maybe something was wrong. "What's with the face?"

Zack jumped. "I'm not making a face."

"You're making a..."

Catching him in a private thought, Zack let other thoughts tumble out. "Mrs. Li must be..."

"Not that! You were making a face!" He started throwing wild gestures at Ellie. "A face... remember?"

"You mean Zack smiling at me?" Ellie chewed on her bottom lip. "Seriously? You're such a — what was the word, Zack?"

"I prefer calling Noah a troglodyte." Fiddling with the table's edge, Zack asked, "What is Mrs. Li doing?"

"I'm making dinner!" Mrs. Li had eagle ears like every other mother Jackson had ever met. "Ellie brings you home, and there is no food!"

"How does Mrs. Li know that?" Jackson whispered. "Is she psychic?"

And clearly, Mrs. Li heard him. "She never has food. I'll make you a hot meal."

Zack pondered more significant questions to stop the furious blushing from his neck to his cheeks. "Why is a Chinese Food restaurant even still open?"

"I'm not dignifying that with a response," Jackson sighed and called out, "Thank you, Mrs. Li."

The phenomenon of Zack's emotions blossoming on his face brought Jackson back to childhood when Zack — and all kids — could acceptably get excited about anything. It had been so many years since Zack showed genuine yet undoubtedly subtle enthusiasm for anything unrelated to the stars.

Three bowls of steaming soup materialize underneath their noses. "Chicken noodle egg drop soup. Warm you right up!"

"Thank you," they all murmured.

The wheel, specifically the third one, started turning. First watching Zack's little emotions emerge from their long hibernation, then formulating a plan to pick up Ellie's mood. Something Jackson still felt he'd crushed in his own way.

The last thing Jackson wanted to do was ruin Ellie and Zack's first Christmas together.

Soup was a hearty first course, but Mrs. Li kept bringing out food, all while muttering under her breath. And as the foods became fattier, he wondered if she was trying to tell all three of them something not so subtly.

After the heavy meal, and somehow against all odds, Ellie and Zack fell asleep on the couch. Ellie took one end of the sofa, furthest from Jackson, placing Zack squarely in the middle. Until the internet went out, they watched a quintessential, classic Christmas miracle movie. By the time the internet service dropped out, Ellie had fallen asleep on Zack's shoulder.

"Don't move her. I'll get the lights turned down," Jackson muttered, walking the perimeter of her studio apartment for the light switch. The overhead lights had two switches, half turned off by one button in the kitchenette and another by the apartment door. But the Christmas lights were a whole other issue. They crisscrossed so many times that Jackson couldn't follow where they ended or started and had zero clue how to turn them off.

By the time he sat back down again, Zack was dozing, gently holding Ellie's hand.

And it made an ache form in Jackson's chest. Part of him totally wanted something like what Zack found. But the other, much more significant part of him was nowhere near ready to settle down. Jackson loved setting off to conventions around the world, writing on the beach in California or the mountains of Colorado for a week. When his budget allowed, usually once or twice a year, depending on how big his novels sold.

Zack and Ellie fell onto Jackson, who was now held hostage by Block. The fur ball found Zack's lap the most comfortable place to sleep in the apartment. A digital photo frame caught Jackson's eye. The pictures cycling through were of Block, Ellie and Block, a few of Ellie and Zack already (that was... surprisingly cute), and people Jackson assumed were Ellie's family. Many pictures had a Christmas theme; it was like she actually updated the photos regularly. And then one popped up of what could have been Ellie's mom and dad, based on what little Jackson could see of the video call earlier, holding a sign that said, "We miss you."

Then another that actually said, "Merry Christmas, Zack & Jackson," in red and green glitter.

God, why were they all so nice? It made him feel even worse about ditching his crazy extended family and screwing up Ellie's holiday.

Realistically, Jackson knew he hadn't truly screwed up their holiday. But there was a growing hole in the pit of his stomach that seemed to differ with him on the facts. Ellie's mood could have been better. Jackson was the variable. The thing that seemed to change her mood.

Giving up on sleep, eventually, Jackson stood, making sure Zack didn't fall over hard enough to wake, and started on a plan.

CHAPTER FOUR

Ellie

She didn't remember falling asleep with a blanket on. Or a mouth full of fur and her hand trapped under Block.

"Mmmpf!" Ellie blew hard to get Block off her and the hair out of her mouth before she accidentally swallowed it. Wrenching free, Ellie pressed up enough to see Zack comfortably asleep, two thin throw pillows under his head.

Her apartment smelled almost like cookies; red, green, and gold twinkled before her. Ellie's eyes adjusted, and bright morning light filtered in, the painful reflection from the snow outside. On her TV was a wonky drawn Christmas tree with a lopsided garland and digitally painted ornaments. Around it, there were a lot of tiny words Ellie couldn't read from her couch.

"Zack? Hey, wake up."

Zack rubbed his eyes, and she felt the familiar graze of his fingers through her hair.

"Where's Jackson?" Ellie asked.

Zack's usual quiet mood in the morning followed her to her apartment. He let her get up and then stood himself, frowning at all the white and gray cat hair all over him. "I need to invest in various cat hair removal tools. That's Jackson's handwriting."

"What is?"

He pointed absently to the screen.

"On the screen. And on your tablet."

Ellie moved to the television and read: '*Twas the night before Christmas, and all through the studio, not a creature stirred, except for Block, who was having a midnight snack. Two people cuddled on the couch; what a sight. Falling in love on a cold winter's night.*

On the kitchen island, which was rather clean by Ellie's standards, were mini pancakes. "Jackson cooked?"

"He's rather good. Dated all the girls in home economics in high school. Usually, the dates followed baking classes."

"Where did he get the ingredients?" Ellie picked one pancake up and tentatively sniffed it. It looked like a pancake and smelled like a pancake.

"Presumably, your landlord. Hopefully, without incident."

Mrs. Li rarely did anything without incident. Ellie grabbed two pancakes for the journey down into the Dragon Palace and dashed out the door in her socked feet. Incidents with Mrs. Li usually involved threats and no more. Still, Mrs. Li had become more protective of Ellie since her kids went to college.

"Mrs. Li?" Ellie ran down the stairs, through the twisty hallway, and into the restaurant that seemed to be perpetually open. "Mrs. Li?"

Laughter came from the back. The kitchen. Ellie moved to run back there, but something caught her arm. "You need shoes." Zack held up a pair of slip-in gym shoes.

"Hey, look who's up!" Jackson bellowed from the Dragon Palace's kitchen entrance.

"Mrs. Li, she isn't... I mean... you're not... is everything okay?"

"I thought laughter was a good sign." Zack's frown deepened, and he considered the last few moments. "I'm confused."

"Mrs. Li is a dream. Merry Christmas!"

Now it was Zack's turn to be cynical, "You hate Christmas."

Jackson ruffled his curls, even after a night of sleeping and all they hadn't flattened or misformed. But then Ellie saw the bags under his eyes and wondered how much sleep Jackson got. "I do. But I guess I realized last night my mood shouldn't impede your and Ellie's Christmas. And it seemed like it had been. So... I'm sorry."

Zack shook Ellie's hand, a sign he wanted to talk, but the stress of social obligations was mounting.

She turned and gave him her full attention.

"I really like you, Ellie, but I don't want you and Jackson fighting constantly. It makes me uncomfortable."

"Zack, I'm sorry. I..." She flicked her eyes back at Jackson and how he hovered over them. And there it was. What grated on her. "I don't think I got over how he... doesn't let you grow and be you."

"Around you?" Zack asked.

"Yes. Like Jackson hovers waiting for you to make a social mistake and correct it or..."

"Or everything around our first few dates?" Zack finished.

"Someone's being protective..." Jackson sang in literally the most grating sing-song voice possible. Like Ellie's teeth started grinding on their own.

"Jackson, that is an unhelpful response." Zack's offhand comment garnered a few chuckles from Jackson.

But he also added, "Pot calling the kettle black and all, my dude."

"I'm not hovering! I'm his..." Ellie tried to stand her ground.

Jackson, though, interrupted with, "You're the woman he's falling in love with. I get it. And..." Jackson met them at the counter, his shirt sleeves rolled up and splatters of oil or butter were evident. "And I know how protective you are because *I* am that protective."

"It's different." Ellie really wondered if Jackson understood the difference.

Jackson's flashy grin, the smile he used to make women fawn over him, faltered. "It's *really* not. Has Zack told you about when we first became friends?"

"I told her we met when we were young. I don't remember how we met."

"Dude, come on. Really?" Jackson knocked Zack's shoulder. "When I asked you out."

Ellie's head jerked at that. "What?" She needed clarification because everything, as in all over the internet, broadcast that Jackson Wolfe went feral over a beautiful woman.

"That wasn't the same." Zack became engrossed in separating his scarf from his coat, which he must have brought down when he brought Ellie's shoes down.

Jackson slapped his face, laughing into his hands. "I literally asked you a date."

Confusion creased Zack's brow. Either from his jacket and scarf or Jackson, Ellie couldn't tell. "It was a movie we were both interested in."

"Yes, we were both interested in it. And I asked you as a *date*."

"I'm not attracted to men," Zack said in his plain monotone, almost like he was distracted.

"I know that *now!* I did not know that then." Frustration shook Jackson's voice.

And Zack added, as if it were not common knowledge (again, broadcast *literally everywhere)*, "You always date women."

"There's not a lot of men in this town that want to date a guy. Especially not our age. Anyway, the point is, *I get it*. More than most.

I get what you're feeling, and I... am sorry. Because I think I'm having a hard time letting go."

Words failed Ellie. Years of following Jackson's career meant she knew a lot about him, but... obviously, only what was put out there on purpose.

"I had no idea..." And now she felt like a complete ass. What a Christmas miracle this was. Another way for Ellie to feel stupid.

"For *years*, Zack has been happy as he is, single. Hanging out with friends and his astronomy stuff. This is all new for him. And for me."

Some small part of Ellie wondered if Jackson had been holding out some hope. In his eyes, she saw a little bit of pain. She couldn't ask but wondered if it was the unrequited kind of pain.

Zack came between them, bundled in his coat and mittens and scarf. Muffled, he asked, "Does this mean it will be more comfortable between you?"

"Yes, Zack," they agreed.

"Where are you going?" Jackson asked, grabbing Zack by the scarf.

"Mom texted for an update. She knows Mrs. Li. She said I should go out and shovel before Mr. Li has a heart attack. Whatever that means."

Ellie found a small patch of Zack's cheek exposed from the scar and kissed him. "I'll help."

"You don't have a coat. That's not a smart..."

"I grew up in the north. I'll be fine. Five minutes at most to shovel out the sidewalk again and salt."

"And," Jackson bowed, "I'll finish the second part of breakfast."

"I need clarification." Zack scrunched up his nose. "How can you tell I'm falling in love with Ellie? I have not come to that conclusion. I feel..."

"Don't need the details, bud. It's how you look at her. I can tell. And you will literally be the last to know. We'll just tell you when it happens." Jackson saw Ellie turn and quickly added, "Ellie can tell you... or... you'll figure it out. I'm working on it, okay?" He gave her a pointed look. "The most Christmas miracle you'll get from me."

AUTHOR NOTES

As an AuDHD mom raising an AuDHD son, there's still so much stigma and tiptoeing around having autism. Like, when we were going for evaluations, so many people were like 'he'll grow out of the hyperactivity,' 'it's just a phase,' or 'he doesn't seem autistic.' Autism feels so overlooked.

In fact, in media, autism doesn't seem to be portrayed often in normal everyday life. So many characters we think are likely autistic (usually, there is nothing explicitly said, but not always) are genius characters that seem too smart to be true (and probably are).

The rise of current social media, though, seems to be stemming the stigma. I wanted to write something where the main character openly is autistic and ends up with the girl. Something my son deals with daily is the struggle of being perceived, of people trying to enforce the neurotypical way things are done socially. Loved ones mean well but many times push what they think is best when it really is just what is most commonly thought to be socially acceptable.